What Would I Tell Her @ 13

SUDESNA GHOSH

HARLEQUIN®

Published in India 2014 by
Harlequin India Private Limited
R - Tech Park, 13th Floor,
Off Western Express Highway
Nirlon Complex Goregoan (E)
Mumbai - 400 063

ISBN 978-93-5106-313-1

Typeset in Times New Roman 11/14 by
InoSoft Systems, Noida

Printed and bound by Thomson Press (India) Ltd.

For my favourite aunt…

About the Author

Sudesna Ghosh is a writer based in Kolkata. Her friends call her Sue. Born in the United States, she moved to India when she was nine. After she finished high school at Calcutta International School, she attended University of Rochester in upstate New York. She chose a psychology major because it would satisfy her obsession with human behaviour and emotions.

Sudesna returned to Kolkata with the plan to pursue a job in advertising or public relations. A few internships later, her obsession with writing began. She started as a freelance writer for the Times of India Group and proceeded to work with The Telegraph newspaper features desk. In between, there was a year of market research but the writing never stopped. Sudesna's features have been published in kolkatamirror.com (now defunct), Education Times, Calcutta Times, timeswellness.com, Careergraph (now relaunched with a different name), Dogs & Pups magazine, Cats & Kittens, and other publications.

She is also a short story writer and has been published in seven Chicken Soup titles. And because she says she will never really grow up, she writes short stories for children. Her stories have been published in TeleKids and other children's magazines across India.

When she isn't writing, Sudesna is busy taking care of her adopted cats and dogs and running a Facebook group for animal welfare and rights.

Contents

Introduction 1

Chapter 1: Hello Independence **9**

Shikha Uberoi's Story 15

Chapter 2: The Power of Confidence **21**

Anjali Raina's Story 27

Chapter 3: Discovering Your Voice **34**

Avantika Akerkar's Story 39

Chapter 4: Newer, Bigger Goals **45**

Meher Pudumjee's Story 51

Chapter 5: The First Crush **57**

Malini Agarwal's Story 63

Chapter 6: Friendship & Cliques **69**

Suhasini Haidar's Story 75

Chapter 7: Staying Safe Offline & Online **81**

Anjali Sharma's Story 87

Chapter 8: Boys Vs. Girls **91**

Komal Sood's Story 97

Chapter 9: Everybody Wants to be Size 0 **102**

Rashmi Uday Singh's Story 107

Ishi Khosla's Story 113

Chapter 10: Choosing Your Role Models 117
Tanusree Shankar's Story 123
Chapter 11: Making Downtime Positive 130
Preeti Vyas's Story 135
SPECIAL FEATURE 143
Fun in the Kitchen with POOJA DHINGRA 143
Chapter 12: Discovering Your Inner Compassion 146
Rimi B. Chatterjee's Story 151
Chapter 13: Terrible Tantrums! 158
Sheena Misra Ghosh's Story 163
Chapter 14: Surviving Child Sexual Abuse 168
Pranaadhika Sinha Devburman's Story 173

Who's Who 180
References 189

Introduction

We've all been thirteen.

You must remember how badly you wanted to reach this milestone. Remember how you craved the freedom to be a semi-grown up? Of course you do. How about those feelings of excitement when your first crush said "Hi!" to you? The memory must make you grin even today.

How about those fights with your mother when you found out that being thirteen wasn't the same thing as being an adult? Ouch. The frown returns. Watching a sweet little girl turn into a melodramatic, moody, insolent child is not easy.

Unfortunately, this is an intrinsic part of the growth process. Thirteen signifies a developing body with heightened hormonal activity which in turn affects daily life and interactions. The activity going on in your teen's body is complex.

An article in the *National Geographic* magazine from October 2011 discussed a study of the adolescent brain conducted by the National Institutes of Health (NIH), USA. The project that studied over a hundred participants, who grew up in the 1990s, showed that our brains undergo a massive re-organisation between twelve and twenty five years of age.

This research tells us that the brain doesn't actually grow much during this period "but as we move through adolescence, the brain undergoes extensive remodeling, resembling a network and wiring upgrade."[1] During this time, the teenager's brain is learning and adapting to new things on its way to adulthood. Every experience is like a lesson that brings her a step closer to having an adult's brain. Scientific observation is a good enough explanation for the intense behavioral and emotional changes we see in our teenagers.

Along with the vacillating moods and preferences, there is the urgent need to discover herself and determine her place in the world. During this mission, parents and sometimes even school work, takes a back seat. You need to be calm and understand that she does not love you any less, but she is just terribly busy trying to feel 'grown up'.

The mother-daughter relationship takes a hit with the closest role model in the house suddenly being viewed as a more powerful member of the same gender. Even the father-daughter bond needs extra nurturing to stay well.

While a mother can be a role model to her daughter with her behaviour, grooming habits and attitude, a father will affect her perception of herself as a woman. What this really means is that praises at dance recitals and letting your little girl know that she is a pretty, loved daughter, needs to come from the father too. In fact, the male parent is your daughter's role model for the opposite sex. Think about him as a template of sorts.

I remember walking through Book Shops and daring to flip through series such as Sweet Valley High and Mills & Boons. The illustrations on the book covers said it all; I wasn't old enough to read them. Older girls and their boyfriends stuck in each other's embrace. Men and women wearing clothes I only dreamt of owning. I hated not being a teenager. My mother

1 *National Geographic Magazine*, http://ngm.nationalgeographic.com/print/2011/10/teenage-brains/dobbs-text, (Date accessed : 28.4.2014)

would see me eyeing the forbidden shelves and direct me towards the detective series. I liked those. But I just couldn't wait to be thirteen so I could read the exciting books.

The older kids I knew in high school had so much more fun than we did. They had crushes that ended up in secret phone conversations when the parents slept. The girls seemed so sure of themselves, flipping their hair with their noses in the air. We worshipped our seniors. Being thirteen seemed such fun! Thirteen was what we wanted to be.

So I did turn thirteen after the painful wait and found myself overwhelmed with anxiety. The older girls back then had made things look easy –when I reached the same age; I realised that they were not. Crushes were not all about feeling happy. My friends and I constantly worried about what the boys thought about us. We scrutinised and analysed every word that came out of our mouths. We debated about the impression we created caused by our every action – whether it was a laugh, or a wave.

Thirteen became synonymous with anxiety.

Attention shifted to breasts and thighs. Suddenly, I noticed that my chest was very different from those of my male classmates. My girlfriends and I started talking about bras and discussing who was too 'small' and envying those who were luckily big.

Before I knew it, the first bra had come into my life. It was a special day for any thirteen-year-old. Remember that day?

I remember how I felt. I remember how I looked. I also recall how odd I felt at school with the new garment that was under my t-shirt but stuck in my mind.

"Can he tell I'm wearing one?" I asked my best friend regarding my current crush. She assured me that he could. Was that a good thing or a bad thing? Well, depended on what my popular girlfriends thought on each specific day. Peers were everything back then.

Alright, I admit that it wasn't all anxiety. There were good moments too. I finally got to read the books that I'd only ever glanced at. There were stories about girls and their boyfriends, stories about teenagers sharing their first kiss. Shelves full of romance, dating and breakups were painfully beyond my reach up until then. These books created more expectations for me. Sleepovers, boyfriends, parties - my friends and I wanted them all. My mother pointed out that the girls in the books lived abroad where certain things were acceptable unlike here in India.

"Thirteen year olds don't walk around with boyfriends here," she had said. Plus, the girls in the books were older sometimes. I didn't give up. Those books kept my thirteen-year-old spirit alive and I began looking forward to turning 16!

I can always relive that day in school when we played Truth or Dare and I got my first kiss (on the cheek). Thirteen was old enough for that first. We all wanted it to be from our first crush and pictured intimate scenes like we had glimpsed on TV, but it was never like that at thirteen. Good, innocent fun that made butterflies dance about in the stomach. My classmates and I thought life should be like it was on Friends. Sitting in a coffee shop, dating good-looking people and wearing stylish outfits – that's what we expected.

With the mix of good, bad and the ugly, thirteen was a growing experience that taught me a lot of what has shaped my personality in my older years. My story was set in the 90s. The life of a thirteen year old girl today is different. A lot has changed. Decades ago, things were even more different. Can you imagine your grandmother at thirteen? Or how about, your great-grandmother?

This book takes you through the lives of some incredible women who reminisce about turning thirteen and being at that tender age as they navigate their personal journeys through tumultuous adolescence. I believe that these stories which are full of emotion, insight and positivity, will help you in your journey. Some of the anecdotes shared will make you cry. Others will cause a laugh or two. A few pages may even make you wonder how the girl in the story became the successful woman she is today.

This book is dedicated to you – the new Indian teenage girl, her parents and anybody else trying to survive this phase. Child psychologists and parents who have passed the milestone don't lie. The Terrible Teens start with an overwhelming bang at thirteen. It's going to be rough. It's going to be tough. But you will be prepared.

In Hello Independence, read and laugh with a young tennis star who tells us about the day that she learnt what Independence was NOT about. Hear from one of India's top journalists as she shares her wisdom gleaned not only from her successful career, but also from her firsthand experience of bringing up her two daughters in today's challenging times.

If you've ever felt like the odd one out in school, you'll be surprised to see how one such little girl became a well-known personality in the fields of theatre and media. In fact, she gives you hope because not fitting in was the reason she became who she is.

Meet an author and professor at Kolkata's leading university. Find out how she discovered her inner compassion and dealt with obstacles along the way.

Hear about a famous danseuse's childhood with her idols and understand the power of having positive examples in your life.

Learn about the dangers that thirteen-year-old girls faced decades ago in an Internet-free world and be relieved that things are safer today. There are new dangers but don't fear when a legal expert and mother is ready to share her advice with you.

Listen to a Child Sexual Abuse survivor and activist as she pours her heart out to you. Self defense skills are needed more than ever before, and her story is there to warn, guide and inspire you.

Take advice from a business leader who has led her teenage daughter to new and bigger goals, without forcing any subject on her.

Hear what a psychologist has to stay about those tantrums that help define teenage years.

There's a lot more to learn about finding success as the book goes on, including a chapter dedicated to a component that is often ignored – hanging loose. Find out why downtime is essential for a healthy teen and pick up interesting suggestions to relax and engage in constructive fun.

Daughters, you need to hear the stories of these amazing women because then you will know why your parents worry about you. But don't worry. This isn't a psychology text book. You'll realise that you aren't the only one having a hard time handling life – your family members are going kind of crazy along with you.

This book isn't all about raising a 'perfect' thirteen-year-old. Letting loose is vital as this well-known entrepreneur will tell you. Well-rounded is the key word here.

I promise that what you will read is your very own go-to book, one that is fit for every young teen girl's parents, teachers, siblings and anybody else who is attempting to understand her. These accomplished women who grew up in different cities and in different periods, have struggled through thirteen and come out shining. They want the same for every thirteen-year-old girl in India. Be enriched by valuable insights and advice from them. Listen to the thoughts of thinkers, doers and believers.

I sign off with a poem that goes best with thirteen.

When you set out for Ithaka
ask that your way be long,
full of adventure, full of instruction.
The Laistrygonians and the Cyclops,
angry Poseidon - do not fear them:
such as these you will never find
as long as your thought is lofty, as long as a rare
emotion touch your spirit and your body.
The Laistrygonians and the Cyclops,
angry Poseidon - you will not meet them
unless you carry them in your soul,
unless your soul raise them up before you.
Ask that your way be long.
At many a Summer dawn to enter
with what gratitude, what joy -
ports seen for the first time;
to stop at Phoenician trading centres,
and to buy good merchandise,
mother of pearl and coral, amber and ebony,
and sensuous perfumes of every kind,
sensuous perfumes as lavishly as you can;
to visit many Egyptian cities,
to gather stores of knowledge from the learned.
Have Ithaka always in your mind.
Your arrival there is what you are destined for.
But don't in the least hurry the journey.
Better it last for years,

so that when you reach the island you are old,
rich with all you have gained on the way,
not expecting Ithaka to give you wealth.
Ithaka gave you a splendid journey.
Without her you would not have set out.
She hasn't anything else to give you.
And if you find her poor, Ithaka hasn't deceived you.
So wise you have become, of such experience,
that already you'll have understood what these Ithakas mean.

Constantine P. Cavafy

Chapter 1

Hello Independence

It is a time of confusion. Your thirteen-year-old is going to oscillate between childish and adult behaviour. This is normal at this age. Get ready to watch her metamorphose from insecure to extra confident, from bored to crazily stimulated, and from secretive to open. You'll be confused for a while as will be your teen, but being thirteen isn't easy. Your daughter expects freedom. Long phone conversations with friends, more time and access to social media, and lots more time to just 'hang out' will become part of her regular existence. The challenge lies in establishing rules which work well for you as well as your daughter.

It is during this time that schools begin to expect students to engage in independent coursework as opposed to parent-supervised projects. Extracurricular activities pave the way for further freedom, giving children more opportunities for socialising with their peers. At home, this new-found freedom needs to be countered with a sense of responsibility. For instance, assigning certain household chores such as cleaning her room every week with no help whatsoever will ensure that she develops into a well-rounded individual.

Some Indian parents think that thirteen is not old enough to help with household chores but their Western counterparts have always set the example of combining freedom with responsibility from a young age. Avoid the common mistake of granting independence with no responsibility. Asking a thirteen-year-old to pitch in with household chores is one way of making her realise that growing up isn't just about fun and friends.

As a conscientious parent, avoid the mistake of helping with homework just because she is cranky or has purposely delayed completing her work on time. Let her do her own homework. Suggest a website to prepare for her school project. But do not draw a map for her. She needs to grow up with your help; not be a spoilt child forever.

At thirteen, your teenager is bound to become emotionally distant from you because of her focus on peer relationships and other anxieties that she has to grapple with. Sometimes, she will want to talk to you. At other times, she will remain locked in her room and act like her life is completely ruined and nobody can understand her.

The concept of having the right to her own space and personal time affects her deeply at thirteen. All of this is normal, as long as it doesn't continue for a long time and affect her daily functioning. In such a situation, a psychologist needs to step in.

In 2011, the journal *Child Development* featured two studies whose results showed that perceptions of peer freedom may predict a teenager's desired levels of autonomy. The first study involved five hundred children in the sixth Grade through to the ninth Grade, and also studied pupils in the twelfth grade.

The second phase of this research studied the same sixth and seventh Grade students when they in a higher Grade.

Both studies were conducted at Ohio State University in the United States. Researchers conducting these studies found out that teenagers used their peers as their social markers to figure out when and in which areas they would like more autonomy.

Another finding highlights how particularly challenging this phase is for girls and observes that "younger teens and girls wanted autonomy more than older teens and boys."

To add to this, researchers found that teenagers consistently overestimate the actual level of independence that their peers have – making the assumption that everybody else has more freedom than they do.

There are the common excuses of trying to give the parents a guilt trip saying, "So and so at school is allowed to stay out until eight o' clock. I'm the only one at school who has to be home so early." Or she may say, "The other girls all have their own phones. I'm the only one who doesn't have one." Parents, now you know that the problem isn't your rules as much as her idea that everybody else is allowed to be more independent than she is.

During this phase in a teenager's life, it is the norm for parents and their children to disagree about independence. A parent has to wonder if he or she is giving her children too much independence too soon. It is natural to worry about trusting your daughter and giving her freedom at an age where she may be too young to make sound judgments and thus may inadvertently compromise on her own safety and well-being.

Things such as early sexual experimentation or smoking for example, need to be prevented through effective guidance. Don't hesitate to let her make a harmless mistake or two because they can teach her what not to do in future when in a similar situation.

There is an art to striking a balance between your own concerns and those of your daughter. Positivity in this challenging phase of life is key to nurturing a happy and successful young person. Keeping your family's cultural background and traditional beliefs in mind, maintain a supportive environment for her. Confidence levels can go from high to low in a moment at this age, so parental shoulders can be step one to building self-esteem. Your child is doing her best to work things out amidst the chaos going through her mind and body. She is striving to answer the question: Who am I?

Some basic ways to build this atmosphere involve giving her space and privacy, recognising her love for you while understanding that she needs to create a place for herself in her peer group. Even though your little girl may not hug you close or show you how much she needs you now, you are still the one who provides emotional direction and strength. So, if she has an opinion that you don't agree with, just share your own and take it as an opportunity to teach her about people agreeing to disagree without hard feelings.

Outlining the family rules about behaviour can help her understand your expectations from her. Consistency is necessary and especially uniformity with other teenagers in the house if your daughter has siblings of either sex. Be careful to draw a line between being too strict and too lenient. Remember that she needs to have new experiences that will promote healthy growth in her mental and physical health. Lack of exposure and too much alone time doesn't make a happy, hardy teenager.

Independence isn't just about having later curfews than before or choosing her own clothes and shoes. Help her become independent by encouraging decision-making. You could start with something small such as asking her to choose a route to school. Another way to boost her feelings of self-worth is to hold a discussion with her regarding the rules. Once you make a decision together, she will know that you respect her feelings and opinions.

Remember that a thirteen-year-old girl is working on forming an identity and fitting in everywhere as an individual. Taking control of socialising and appearance are primary aims which parents can be seen to be obstacles too, so no amount of freedom may seem enough. She might even question authority figures including you and her teachers.

However, don't let the notion that all teenagers are rebellious and unpleasant make you feel stressed. Your teen is still close to you and loves you. Think of this time as a stage where many adjustments will take place. Some girls may make their peers' value system their own. Others may struggle to conform to family values while adapting some aspects of their peers' beliefs. There isn't much reason to worry since this is temporary – just like every other part of this new beginning.

Shikha Uberoi's Story

13

When I was twelve and on the verge of becoming a teenager, I remember being anxious. The good part about this was the fact that being thirteen would enable me to start playing professional tennis. It also meant that I could compete in World Tours. The bad part was that I also worried about people thinking that I was nine and not thirteen because of the way I looked. When you're that age, I think you really get to notice who the pretty girls in class are and if you're one of them or not. I wasn't one of them.

Even though I was a social butterfly and friends with everyone, I didn't really fit in with the pretty girls at school. I used to say "hi!" to them and try and be friends with them, but they got too boring for me. We didn't have girly magazines, nail polish or jewellery at home, so I couldn't relate to most of what they talked about.

There is one challenge that I was glad to not have thrown at me, but which I find increasingly common these days. It is society's tendency to objectify women and young girls and look at them through a hyper sexualised lens. Little girls are completely surrounded by messages which tell them that they must look a certain way in order to be desirable. Cell phones, the internet and TV keep reinforcing gender stereotypes and it is scary that there is not much one can do to block out this flood of objectification.

Indian girls need realistic, healthy heroes or 'sheroes'. I feel that girls are restricted to just two options; to either be the dumb, good looking female, or the super bright leader who everyone envies or fears. There are not enough examples where a woman can be smart, feminine and a leader in her field. Thirteen-year-old girls need role models who say, "Hi. I'm beautiful, powerful and brilliant, and people respect me and see beyond what I look like".

On the other hand, recent diets are affecting teens with childhood obesity. Thirteen-year-olds are often terribly overweight and this affects their health making them susceptible to diabetes which hinders their emotional growth as well. This in turn has a serious impact on their sense of self and self esteem, often spilling over to adulthood. It's quite a scary thing to see childhood obesity hit India directly alongside malnutrition and extreme poverty.

Along with that, I feel that that now, more than ever, the fixation with status symbols plaguing the teen is responsible for the philosophy that only material things lead to success and happiness. There is nothing worse a parent can do than encourage such an idea because elements like empathy and compassion are usually ignored in the process.

Thankfully, I grew up free from all of those problems, and thus, could appreciate all things and focus on success and progress in every sphere of my life. Mental success, physical health and career goals were all family values. From what everyone tells me, I was always an independent, self-reliant child. In fact, when I was twelve years old, my father, along with my sister Neha and I, moved to Florida so that Neha and I could pursue our professional tennis career dreams. My mother didn't join us. It was a big change and a challenge.

In Florida, the three of us found ourselves living in a competitive jungle. Nobody seemed to want to believe that two skinny little Indian girls, who looked much younger than their age, had a chance to even be on the same court with tall, well-developed Americans and Russians, let alone make it on the professional WTA[1] Tour.

At home and in 'school', I quickly became Neha's mother, best friend and older sister, all at once. Therefore, 'Independence' descended upon me with extended responsibility in my new life, in a new location. I was responsible for my wins, my losses, my actions and words, and for my kid sister's well being too. In some way, I felt like an adult.

But if I were to look back and pinpoint the one defining moment of independence at the time, it was with my mother. We were at a party when I decided to look for her. Somebody told me that my mother was sitting outside on the steps. That was strange, I thought. She's usually right in the middle of the party, enjoying herself with all the other ladies, sipping never-ending cups of tea. So, I went outside to talk to her.

She looked sad sitting there alone. More than sad, she looked scared. I sat down next to her. She may have been holding off tears but she turned and looked me directly in the eye. She asked, "Are you sure you want to go to Florida and play professional tennis?" I remember pausing before I answered with confidence, "Yes." That one affirmative was what she wanted to hear from me before my dream would split up our family for nearly eight years. The silent hug that followed that short conversation signified the beginning of independence that would include major responsibility.

1 Women's Tennis Association

I'll share a story that depicts how independent and cool I thought I was until my parents burst my bubble. I remember a boy at the tennis academy who was a bit younger than me but definitely cooler than I was because all the older kids liked him. He used to use swear words a lot. At that point, I thought he sounded liberated and cool.

So, I thought I'd try the 'F bomb' (saying the f word out loud) for the first time. But I thought that the first time I wanted to drop the F bomb had to be really special. I wanted lots of people to notice it and me. The plan was to be executed in front of the older kids group because I thought that they needed to see this cool version of Shikha. Unfortunately, things didn't work out according to plan.

I had decided to do it during afternoon tennis practice - and when my dad wasn't watching. The coast was clear. I was ready for action. Halfway through the practice session, I missed another backhand in the net and loudly said the "f" word. I found the last letters choking on themselves. But, I had technically said it. Snapping out of my trance, I looked around and saw curious looks on one or two big kids' faces.

My coach had a puzzled look on his face. Yes, I was sure that the message had been delivered. But whatever progress I thought I had achieved was quickly dampened by my father marching onto the court! I recall thinking, "Where had he been hiding all this while?" From the look on his face and his giant steps, I knew it. I was in trouble. My father had heard me. Even the older kids ran away from the spot.

Dad was livid. He came over to me and looked into my eyes. He asked me, "What did you say?" For the life of me, I couldn't lie. And lying right to his face would be impossible. So, giving up any chance of being a cool teenager, I admitted, "I said the F-word." He glared at me and walked off the court. When I got home that day, a giant stack of paper and a pencil were waiting for me. I was brought back to my earlier childhood years as I began to write out "I will not curse" numerous times.

While I was suffering through my punishment, my little sister was sitting across the table, happily eating her dinner, oblivious to what I was doing, swinging her dangling legs. She was so short that her legs didn't even touch the floor. Her glasses covered most of her face. And then with everything else in that scene, Neha's silly grin got to me. Suddenly, I felt like I had regressed to something even younger than my kid sister. Wow, I had been stupid.

That is when I realised what independence was not about. The reality is that a thirteen-year-old girl needs to use her independence to her advantage. In other words, the first step would be to use her independence to add to her skills, her social development, and her personal growth. Thirteen is a great time to take forward passion and talent that exists in any area.

In turn, this is the ideal time to start converting these emotions and motivation into skill sets and investment for the future. For example, if a girl is interested in photography, she could take her cell phone and create art or ask to be enrolled in photography classes. Other examples of this kind of independence could be leadership roles in mentoring positions and volunteering time to organisations, or even babysitting.

One important piece of advice for parents: Give children the freedom to choose for themselves! There is definitely a fine line between control and guidance that many parents unwittingly fail to adhere to, quite frequently. This is why extreme teenage rebellion occurs, often followed by a lack of communication. It is harmful when parents live vicariously through their children, forcing them to not only go to dance, tennis, piano, tuitions, but also by insisting that they finish at the top in each of the activities they pursue.

Often, they never even ask if the child wants to engage in any of those activities. The moment children in this situation feel slightly independent, they jump at the opportunity, pushing it to its extreme. It's a natural reaction and I don't blame the kids. The saddest thing about this, is that even if they succeed at each of their efforts, they have really only fulfilled their parents' expectations and desires, not their own. So the self confidence you would expect such an overachiever to have is not even owned by the child, it all belongs to the parents.

Understand that choice empowers children. It makes them feel good about their value on earth. In addition to that, they like you more for giving them this freedom. It is amazing how easy it is to get through to children this age by simply asking them "how are you feeling?" or "do you want to do X or Y?" The idea is to raise a young, beautiful person who is entirely her own person.

When you allow this independence, a leader is born. The great thing about that is that leaders feel empowered. They have a lot of self confidence because they have had choices and believe in their ability to make the right ones. No one has done everything for them. Instead, it has been their independence and freedom of thought that has contributed towards building their self worth and success.

Responsibility is inherent to independence because it is the driving force that reinforces the fact that independence comes at a price. Independence in my family is earned. It's never assumed. A person will always be accountable for her actions, so independence is better earned, rather than allowed just because a certain age has been reached.

Chapter 2

The Power of Confidence

Urban India has witnessed a lot of changes in the last decade, but some things remain the same. So, thirteen-year-old girls are still victims of oscillating confidence levels. Even with the gains in education and employment opportunities throughout the country, our girls cannot escape the effects of raging hormones and social pressure that leaves nobody's daughter untouched. If the sudden lows and lack of highs scare you- the parent-don't worry. This kind of behaviour is normal. Of course, normal is not a synonym for easy.

Confidence is a powerful feeling that is tangled with a range of emotions for the young teenager. It can make or break any person - especially a child at this vulnerable stage of her life. A girl who does not master the skills required to adjust to these new settings, is likely to develop what famous psychologist Erik Erikson called a "sense of inferiority".

Subsequently, this can lead to long-lasting intellectual, emotional, and interpersonal issues throughout her teens and even adulthood. Researchers in the United States have substantiated Erikson's view.

Indeed, feelings of competence and personal value are of central importance for your daughter's well-being.

In an article published by The Future of Children (USA), Jacquelynne S. Eccles, a professor, discusses several factors which contribute to a drop in confidence. She explains that as children grow older, they receive more feedback about failure than before. With more to prove to themselves and their peers, they become more able to reflect on their performances and compare those with how the other children are performing. The young teenager suddenly learns that "current failures are likely to be clues to future performance."

Parents, there's hope for you if you accept that her self-confidence will behave like a yo-yo. The first step is making a list of things that boost her confidence. The common list should include: making friends with the popular children at school, making new friends at extracurricular activities that she takes part in, feeling pretty, getting to hear the latest gossip about breakups and new couples and seemingly small things like a popular boy sending her a Facebook friend request. Seeing that a popular boy click 'like' on her status update can make a huge difference to her day. Teens can even feel very insecure when they compare the number of Facebook friends each of them have.

Don't make the mistake of telling your daughter that social life and being liked is not important. Just think about her spending all day in school, surrounded by other children who are stressed out about the same things. It is hard for her. Family members and teachers can expect trouble if they believe that they can keep the girls isolated from such challenges. No thirteen-year-old is above it all.

Once you recognise her natural situation, dealing with it

can be simpler. Simpler - not easy. This means that you cannot make your daughter stay home when all of her friends are at the movies having a great time. Well, you cannot keep her locked in every time there's a social event that she actually does need to go to.

Along with the constant need to impress, your little girl's attention has shifted to her changing body. Self-esteem and her confidence depend on what she thinks, or rather, what she thinks that everybody else thinks, about her new physical appearance. Sometimes, this focus is more destructive when adults and media such as movies, suggest that being a girl is all about the looks. There's the dangerous bunch who insist that intelligent girls are not attractive. This in turn, leads to little girls hiding their accomplishments. The straight 'A' students are almost immediately nicknamed 'nerds'. You see what these young girls are subjected to? No wonder they are so stressed out and difficult at times.

There is a silver lining though. Unsteady confidence levels and broken confidence can be repaired. The girls need to be assertive instead of being silent in fear of people laughing at them. When she needs to talk about something, she has to speak up. If she stands her ground with her peers, they will take her confidence into account and will think twice before picking on her.

In fact, a confident child can respond to a peer who is hurting her feelings by saying: You are not being nice to me. I don't like it. Or, if a troublemaker at school asks her to join along with creating trouble, she can tell the person that she does not want to be involved in the endeavour. Basically, the thirteen-year-old girl can pick up tips on how to speak with confidence, protecting her well-being in the process.

Parents and educators can help in other ways too. Compliment her on her appearance. She will love to hear about her hair looking nice and her new earrings being beautiful, but be sure to praise non-appearance aspects as well. For instance, when you attend your daughter's school play, praise her acting skills. While that kind of praise goes a long way in affecting a girl's confidence, do not overdo it. An overconfident teen can mess up things because she thinks she is better than everybody else around her. Nobody likes overconfident peers who make a fool of themselves when they have to prove their real abilities.

Think about a girl who thinks she is good enough to be a doctor just because her parents are both doctors. Then the girl stops paying attention to her academic life because she assumes she is automatically qualified to be a doctor. That can never be good! Then there are the times when peers won't ask her to participate in social activities with them. Most classes have a clique or two that only spends time together and makes a point of making everybody else feel left out. Adults can spell out reality because the damaged confidence can be reversed when she gets it into her head that the problem is not with her – but with the other children's' behaviour. As she gets older, she will find out herself that everyone cannot like everyone enough to hang out together.

Confidence also comes from knowing what she is capable of doing. Homework is a start. Don't help her as soon as she asks because that can become a habit and she is the one who will end up feeling incompetent. She needs to try harder. Adding art classes or sports classes or even volunteer work to your daughter's schedule is wise. For those who think that girls shouldn't play sports, you'll only hinder her self-confidence if you tell her that she will not be able to play one. Let her find out for herself what she is good at and bad at.

Last but not least, don't forget that teenagers pick up a lot of their behaviours and tastes from people they see around them. This includes TV sitcom characters, popular girls in school, actresses and sometimes, their own mothers or older sisters. In this scenario, positive female role models can play a role in developing her confidence. Let her read articles about these women. If these women come to your city for an event, take your child along.

It isn't just role models, teachers, parents and peers who the thirteen-year-old needs to interact with. Talking to acquaintances is vital to building her confidence. Next time you take her to the neighbourhood grocer, hand the money to her and instruct her to ask for the items herself. By the time she counts the money, takes the change, and walks out of the store with the groceries, she will feel more grown up and confident.

Anjali Raina's Story

I turned thirteen a long time ago – over 43 years ago! No wonder that when I tried to recall what it was like to finally be a teenager, I had to refer to my journals to refresh my memory. I have kept a journal since I was eleven years old, but this is the first time that I revisited them. Once I started reading my memories, I couldn't stop. Each entry in my journals brought back so many emotions. They reminded me of the intensity of being thirteen, the delirious joy of friendship found and returned, and the deep despair associated with an unfair outcome.

It also made me relive the enjoyment of hard won achievement and the curiosity about happenings in the wider world. All of this was covered with a dreamy sense of wonder. I remember being preoccupied with philosophy and the meaning of life, accompanied by selfish absorption in petty concerns and a very adult interest in the world around me.

It was an interesting time. Indira Gandhi swept the polls in 1971 with her '*Garibi Hatao*' campaign, bulldozed the creation of Bangladesh out of the former East Pakistan, and signed the Simla agreement with the Pakistani PM Zulfikar Bhutto. She was a powerful role model. Till then my ambitions had been to be a nurse or an airhostess- to play second fiddle to the 'male' doctor or pilot.

When I read about the two most powerful women in South Asia - Indira Gandhi in India and Sirimavo Bandaranaike in Sri Lanka, I began to listen to my father's advice to think beyond the books I was reading. My reading list back then included books like The Shirley Flight Airhostess series and the Cherry Ames Student Nurse series.

I started reading magazines such as Newsweek and Time. They kept my interest alive in events taking place around the world - which seemed to all be about conflict. The year 1971 began with the hijacking of the Indian airlines plane 'Ganga' to Lahore by two Kashmiri militants, and through 1972 there were a series of nuclear tests by the US, France and USSR.

Then, there was the carnage of the Vietnam war and the unending animosity in Northern Ireland. The Munich Olympics were marred by the tragedy of the murder of 11 Israeli athletes. So, war seemed to be a fact of life. In fact, my cousins and friends and I played bloodthirsty war games –variations of team hide and seek -where the aim was to 'kill' the opposing team.

But there were good memories as well. I followed United States President Nixon's visit to China, the end of the Vietnam War in December 1972, and the triumph of Bobby Fischer in chess. The conversations around these events at our dinner table at home led to the belief that the art of communication and an understanding of different cultures was the key to world peace. I also learnt that the civilised way to express conflict was through a game like chess, and not the kind of games that we had been playing.

I felt that at thirteen, I would enter a magical world and the stress and strain of being a tween would vanish. Sadly, I exchanged the playful world of childhood for a rather stressful entry into the teenage years. I loved school because even after three years of struggle with a new school, critical peers and difficult coursework, I managed to come into my own and shot to the top of the class. I made a series of best friends in school and in my neighbourhood.

Along the way, I discovered the joy of being considered pretty. Yes, I was the proverbial ugly duckling who blossomed at thirteen.

However, the unaccustomed sense of achievement created its own stress. Having tasted the pleasure of being ranked number one, I was scared to lose my position. This ensured that I worked very hard to stay ahead, sacrificing some of the dreamy relaxed approach I had become used to. I also selfishly made time for some friends and not others.

I dreamt of being a writer. But when I grew up, I became a banker. Life takes strange twists and turns, because after 25 years in the world of finance, I moved to Harvard Business School as the Executive Director of the India Research Centre and found myself in a job that involves writing!

The challenges of being thirteen revolved around being connected to your friends. School was far from home, so meeting school friends after school was over for the day, or on weekends, was difficult. Leisure activities were mostly outdoors because there was no TV, Internet, or video games. Board games required company. There was only one telephone, and that too, a landline. Speaking for more than a few minutes on the phone wasn't allowed unless it was on the pretext of doing homework.

The challenge was to 'manage' our parents and permissions, so that we girls could meet our friends. I remember that when I finally acquired the permission to walk by myself to my friend's home in the neighbourhood and to cycle over to meet others, it opened a whole new world of fun and friendship. Some of those friendships are alive even today. The interconnected world facilitates friendships for today's thirteen-year-old in so many ways.

The battle for permission remains but permission is needed to access the latest device - the mobile, the iPad, or the computer. The issue of course is that friendships seem to be virtual in every sense. A large quantity but somewhat shallow number of friendships seems more common these days.

At home, my relationship with my mother wavered between hero-worship and open animosity. We disagreed about everything. My friends, what I did in my leisure time, my clothes and how I managed my time, were all topics of heated argument. Through those rocky times, I learned that constant conflict in a relationship is tiring and leads to much unhappiness.

On the other hand, my relationship with my younger sister was a source of comfort and strength. She was and still is my best friend. I can count the number of times I have fought with her on the fingers of one hand. I make every effort for harmony and try to keep relationships going under all circumstances.

Another lesson from being thirteen taught me that a curious mind and a great sense of imagination are the best company and ways to cure loneliness and boredom. Reading voraciously, asking questions, and making connections, has helped me grow my mind and personality, and keep me grounded. I was blessed with inspiring teachers. Over the years I have tried to share this love of learning with people around me. Transforming those I am in touch with, helping them reach their potential, like I was helped to reach mine, makes me feel fulfilled.

During my childhood, I learned that being generous and

giving time and support to the less fortunate is important. My family and I had so much and found ourselves surrounded by poverty in Kolkata. Triggered by this observation, I volunteered my time and energy to help those less privileged whenever I could.

Working at Mother Teresa's orphanage was an eye opening experience. I learned to be grateful for what I had, and to share what I could. I became interested in religion, spirituality and meditation, and still draw strength from this. Then there was the time when I developed jaundice and it took me six months to completely recover. I learned the significance of having a healthy body. That's when I developed my love for yoga.

I discovered that a positive outlook, hard work and persistence can defeat all odds, and this laid the foundation for my disciplined approach to balancing the demands of work, home, family and relaxation. Living this way makes each day happy and full of confidence for me.

I think being popular is definitely important to a thirteen-year-old girl. However, I found that I needed it less when I was thirteen than when I was twelve. When I turned thirteen excelling at my schoolwork seemed the most important thing to me. Friends seemed to follow. Boyfriends didn't really matter. There were a few shy explorations, but in general the boys I knew seemed immature and uninteresting.

Looking good began to matter- and I began taking more interest in personal grooming, and clothes. If I had to choose however, I would prioritise schoolwork over a visit to the beauty salon. I suppose that was because I was in an all girls' school and the opposite sex wasn't a daily presence in my life. There was peer pressure to 'lighten up' but for some reason I resisted it. Perhaps I enjoyed the thrill of learning too much to care about anything else.

I returned to school two weeks after the school year had

begun in January 1972, as there were labour problems in Kolkata where we lived, making it unsafe for my younger sister and me to be there.

This was unusual, as our school didn't permit such leave of absence. I received a chilly reception from the class teacher, who hadn't been briefed on the reason for my absence and was not happy about the extra work involved in bringing me up to speed. I made matters worse by responding in a casual way to her questions.

We certainly started off on the wrong foot. Thankfully, a few days of hard work brought me back to where my classmates were already, and I did quite well in the next test. The teacher was surprised and praised me. This raised my confidence levels. My self-confidence was reinforced further when I scored well in an all India examination. Finally, there was validation that I was intelligent. I loved being known as a smart girl.

Another incident that made my confidence levels soar occurred when one of my mother's friends undertook the responsibility to see that I was well-groomed. My hair and nails were taken care of and I suddenly started looking good. I stopped avoiding looking at myself in the mirror and acknowledged that I wasn't bad looking after all. Yet, my constant fights with my mother over the issue of independence, took away from my spirit until I just learned to be more tactful. Confidence is powerful.

When a girl believes in her own capabilities, she can stand strong. Parents can help a thirteen-year-old explore, develop and recognise her talents and skills. You must support her dreams and praise her achievements - that is the key to building her confidence. But be realistic in your praise and expectations. Instead of creating a self obsessed overconfident child, encourage new activities where she can try out new skills that she never knew existed. A balanced self image rooted in reality is a strong foundation for success in life.

Now that I look back at those days, I realise that I never understood my parents' fears for my safety. As I read my diary and reflect on the pressures of raising my own daughter, I have far more sympathy for my mother and father and the rules that they had set for me. I have approached the challenge of parenting by attempting to keep my daughter safe by sharing all possible dangers with her, while helping her make choices wisely. In the process, her confidence gets built but innocence is destroyed. It's a tough call. Still, just like most things in life, being a teenager has its share of good and bad. So enjoy being thirteen. It is a special time.

Chapter 3

Discovering Your Voice

Today's teenager is constantly bombarded with content. The content being mentioned here refers to messages or information from books, magazines, television shows, role models, parents, teachers and even the environment she is exposed to every day. The thirteen-year-old has a lot to observe and a lot to selectively take in or ignore. In other words, all of these elements in her daily life are bound to contribute to her voice. It doesn't happen in a day or a week. It will take time, but when she discovers her voice, her desires will be a sum of her experiences and interactions.

While parents and educators cannot really control what the girls are doing all the time, there are ways to help her expand her horizons. Inculcating a reading habit is one such step. Not only will reading books add to her vocabulary, but the plot, characters and themes can teach her about a life she has no idea about.

In fact, The Organisation for Economic Co-operation and Development (UK) conducted a study on teenagers that resulted in the conclusion that getting teenagers to read for pleasure is of pivotal importance. The research suggests that those who read for pleasure show a desire to engage with stories, texts are known to display more enthusiasm for learning. This translates to an attraction and habit of learning and not just a love for books. Unfortunately, researchers have found that unlike British boys and girls, Indian boys have more positive attitudes to reading than Indian girls do. It is up to you, the parents, to influence and encourage your daughters to read more and inculcate in them the habit of reading books.

Help her choose books at the bookstore or library. She shall likely want to read books with characters that she can identify with – young girls, trying to find the perfect boyfriend and worrying about being popular. She may want to read stories with female protagonists who are older as well. These girls are who she aspires to be. Those with an interest in mystery may choose series based on female detectives who save the day and have great friends and boyfriends too.

Parents, your job isn't to put those books back on their shelves. Instead, let her explore her interests. Additionally, you can suggest other reading material that will create new interests for her. For example, subscribing to National Geographic magazine could spark an interest in animals. This, in turn, could someday lead to her choosing a profession that highlights her compassion- perhaps an animal rights activist or a vet.

By encouraging her, you are showing her that you have full faith in what she is choosing to pursue. If you think, she is making a mistake, guide her but be gentle. Teenage years are tender. You need to gradually earn the faith and trust of your teenager. By being patient and listening to her, you could learn several new things in the process. Maybe her mistakes will remind you of your own teenage years and may find yourself becoming extremely patient as the teenage journey continues. If her reading list includes books that have strong female protagonists who display independence and scientific genius, your teen may start thinking about the possibility of being in this woman's shoes a few years later.

There are other activities that can provide the push she needs to put all thoughts in one place. School dramas, debates and extempore contests will ensure that she builds confidence. At a time in their lives where the girls are often shy because they are so scared of making a wrong move or creating a bad impression in front of their peers, these are methods to get her to speak out and think about life beyond school.

If the thought of public speaking scares her too much at first, a simple conversation with adults can help broaden her mind and challenge her attitude. There was a time in India when women couldn't even look men in the eye, but that has changed in urban, cosmopolitan India.

A father or uncle or aunt can sit down with his daughter, discuss interesting topics or ask her for her opinions on things outside the textbook. Who knows, she may want to know more about something that had never crossed her thoughts before? Either way, holding a conversation with an adult is a challenge for the teen and can improve her confidence too.

Your daughter's search for her voice is an exploration that should answer the 'why' of what she wants to do. This goes beyond thinking about her future career. When she discovers her voice eventually, she will know why she is unique.

Although she's not that old in terms of years, the thirteen-year-old girl is quite perceptive. There are moments that will guide her to discovering her voice. Think about her skills. Now is the time when she will become more aware of what she is good at and what she can do best with no help from adults.

Her aptitude may lie in drawing. She could find herself helping classmates with their lessons so often that it may hit her: I would make a good teacher. Another child may discover that she plays badminton so well that it could be a bigger part of her life than just a leisure activity.

Emotions can be another source of discovery. A teen can spend hours watching TV or listening to adults talking around her, but it is only some information that will affect her enough to think and reflect.

Identifying what makes her feel sad, what makes her feel happy and what makes her want to get up and change the world, is all about her voice. There will be scenes from the news channel playing in the living room, that will make her cry and ask you about terrorism, drought or poaching.

Realising what makes her feel angry is another part of the discovery. Learning about an incurable disease that killed a family member could lead her to studying science and being passionate about finding a cure. Anger stemming from a badly cooked meal can create a food writer or chef – or a girl who works in the field of nutrition maybe?

Once again, it isn't all about the career. Her voice spreads over her entire personality and attitude. Spending time as a volunteer at a local old age home could stir compassion that sticks to her forever. A summer break spent helping out at an animal shelter could create a lifelong decision to always speak out for animals in need. She could exchange just a few words with somebody at a writing workshop, but these words could stay ingrained in her. Precious time spent with her grandparents could teach her about the struggle of being a woman in older India and make her strive towards a role that she wishes her grandmother could have played.

The thirteen-year-old will eventually discover her voice with your help. Just don't expect every girl her age to have the same voice. Only she will know what she is meant to be and meant to do. Be there for her. Guide and suggest. Do not attempt to force her. Let her enjoy the journey.

Avantika Akerkar's Story

I remember feeling a lot of peer pressure when I turned 13. I believe that a lot of it was because my girlfriends at school starting discussing new things about life. Through these conversations, I learnt that thirteen was the age that you started menstruating and when your body started changing since you were starting some phase called the teens. Being an early bloomer, my body had already started experiencing changes from my tenth year. So, I wasn't really sure about what all the sudden fuss was about. And I faced anxiety because I didn't start menstruating until I was 15.

That left me with angst ridden years after thirteen and I ended up thinking that something was wrong with me. Where were my periods? While I didn't have the opportunity to share the excitement of those changes with the other girls in class, there was a new-found awareness in terms of boys. Suddenly, I was constantly conscious about the fact that boys and men were looking at me. I could feel their eyes on me. My parents encouraged my brother and myself to be open and share with the family, so turning thirteen translated into sharing more problems with them – problems that confused me.

When I reflect on those days, I see a different scene for thirteen-year-olds back then. Life is incredibly different now than when I was growing up. In fact, my teenage years were so innocent. There were no technological influences that altered behaviors, peer pressure was somehow different and less complicated, and societal influences were different. For example, I remember being able to wear shorts and t-shirts and taking public transportation on my own in such outfits and my parents wouldn't think twice about it.

Today, I notice how men look at my thirteen-year-old nieces when I walk down the street with them, and it scares me. Mumbai doesn't seem as safe as it used to be. I try to share my concern with my nieces by telling them that although they shouldn't become conscious about what they wear, they need to be conscious of and responsible about their safety the moment that they step outside the security of their homes. Ignoring strangers who try to talk to them, calling in at home with their whereabouts, and traveling in a group; these are just some things that I advise them about.

Along with educating young teens about safety, sex education is important too. Actually, when I became alert about the presence of boys around me and how they were interested in me, I shared my feelings with my mother. As I told her about everything, she realised that it was time to share the facts of life with me. Honestly, she had tried to sit me down for that lecture at a younger age, but I was not ready to listen then. Being a tomboy who wasn't conscious about her body until that's all everybody talked about, I had not shown any interest.

My mother surprised me with her frankness. We looked at books that my grandmother (her mother) used to teach her from. Even though the books were in German and from a very different generation, my mother used them as a reference point. Adding to the facts, she shared her own experiences with me. We giggled a bit. We were serious for a bit. The discussion involved understanding what it meant to become a woman in every sense of the term. After that day, I gained confidence and self-respect that had been absent before. I'm thankful to my mother for helping me reach my goal of being comfortable with my body and feelings.

Other than goals related to coping with this new phase of life, there was the time that I had to overcome challenges in my education. I went to a school that was based on the Montessori system of dialogue, project learning (precursor to the present IB system), and discussion. The teachers began to give us homework only when I was in the 5th grade. I was always a great student and never had a problem coping with the changing academic system or with the new workload.

The problem arose when my school switched over to the Maharashtra State Education board. I was unhappy. Having grown up in a house that encouraged questioning and dialogue, and, subsequently, in a school that had encouraged the same, this was a big blow to the way I looked at the world. The new system was based on rote memorisation that emphasised a student's ability to memorise books without looking at the aspect of understanding. In that situation, I faced a major conflict in my mind. I was often in the library, skipping class because I wasn't learning a thing. Sometimes, I was thrown out for asking too many questions. The misery ended when I was admitted to a boarding school whose curriculum was based on the system of open dialogue, discussion and projects that I was used to. I was back on track.

I don't think that I really ever consciously wrote out my goals. Instead, I remember taking things one day at a time, dealing with everything that came my way, be it good or bad. I am not sure if I was able to process well enough the painful things that happened, but I did develop various coping mechanisms that allowed me to be as strong as I could be at that age. My classmates were not particularly pleasant or kind and would gang up on me because I was one of the 'foreigners' in class; my mother is European and my father is Indian. I didn't understand why they would do something like that. So, I guess you could say that one of my major goals at that time of high peer pressure was to please my classmates and stop them from troubling me.

I was never the sort to be a part of cliques. That made life hard for me in school as being a young teen requires one to be a part of a group, clique or gang. The truth was I enjoyed my own company a lot - something that I still enjoy in my adult life. I hated gossiping and being mean to others to impress close friends or boys. I even recall that one of the rites of passage for one particular gang of girls at school was to demonstrate loyalty by being mean to non-group members. I failed at this and found myself an outsider most of the time. I suppose that my habit of staying to myself is a reason that I have been good at solving my own problems down the years, instead of depending on anybody.

My individualistic nature was further developed a few years later when my parents said that my brother and I could experiment with cigarettes and alcohol if we wanted to but only if we felt the desire to and not egged on by peer pressure. My parents also encouraged us to try new things, to challenge ourselves and stand up for what we thought was injustice or an infringement on our rights. This was further enhanced in me when I lived in New York City for 15 years, and a total of 17 years in the States. I grew up with no pressure to conform to what everybody else was doing, or to prove something to anyone except myself.

My endless alone time allowed me to look at life from a different perspective. Staying away from unhealthy peer pressure, I was not easily impressed by the things that made the others excited. People with money, fancy cars, nice houses – these did not interest me, while girls and boys around me were busy showing off their parents' wealth. In fact, I remember a boy who tried to woo me with his foreign car – which was a huge thing in India in the 1970s. He gave me little gifts too.

Then one day I saw him ill-treating his household help and knew that this boy was not worth my time or feelings. I continue to feel the same way about money and people's behaviour and attitude associated with it, even today. I don't chase money. I focus on having what I need to live with no complaints. I value people according to how they are as human beings. In addition to choosing to not interact with superficial people, I remember spending a lot of time with animals. They were uncomplicated and loving.

Although most of my goals in my early teens were oriented towards overall personal development and satisfaction, failure was a big issue with me. I never allowed myself to fail at anything. Highly competitive, I had to win. There was no other option. I admit that this characteristic got me into trouble and often depressed me. Whether it was academics or sports, I wouldn't be happy until I was the best. And this had to be recognised by everybody else to make the win worthwhile. There were times when I insanely happy. But when I didn't win, I reacted strongly. This behavior crept into my college experience and it took me a while to get over it.

I was lucky to have such wonderful parents. A thirteen-year-old girl needs a parent who will stop everything he or she is doing and LISTEN. Making themselves available to their girls is important. I think that most children have a hard time becoming teenagers, but compared to boys their age, girls develop faster mentally, emotionally and physically. I tell my teen nieces that it is okay to feel inadequate, insecure and unsure about things. It's like a rite of passage for all of us, including the parents. Parents need to be open and straightforward, sharing their personal examples to teach their daughters how to cope (and how not to cope) with this transition. The more available they are, the stronger a support system it will be, helping the teen find her own voice.

Encourage her to continue her education, if she is privileged enough to have an education, and to try to find a mentor who will guide her. I think that children desperately need a good mentor to guide them. I would also encourage her to spend time with her friends, but to put in perspective that she may not have all the opportunities her friends have, and that it is okay to be different. I would also ask her to write a diary to share those intimate things that she can't share with an adult, in order to vocalise her concerns and fears.

Another bit of advice I would give is to encourage exposure to girls from different parts of the world and from various backgrounds to truly understand that the world is a wonderfully diverse place and she is one of the many unique little girls in it. Thanks to the Internet, she doesn't need to travel across the globe to meet these girls. It could be as simple as connecting her to a pen pal who she can reach by letter or email, or enrolling her in foreign language classes as an extracurricular activity. With all the effort, she will certainly discover her unique voice.

Chapter 4

Newer, Bigger Goals

As girls enter their teens, they want to take over the world. Being popular in school, having good grades to show for her achievements and excelling at extracurricular activities –all of these become her priorities. During this time, she wants to be a winner in every area of her life. Before thirteen, her goals were probably smaller and ever changing. The teen years may start out with fickle planning, but steady goals make their way in soon. As the girls explore with a brain that is busy adapting higher capabilities to process information and life in general, goals continue to change but become bigger in a way.

Your daughter's goals can be long-term or short-term. The long-term goals are her objectives which she wishes to fulfill over a considerable period of time. For instance, her desire to write a book by the time she starts college could be her long-term goal.

A child determined to finish her current project over the weekend is someone who is focusing on her short-term goals.

Your teenager is bound to have a set of goals that contain a mix of both kinds of goals. She will have academic goals, social and emotional goals, extra-curricular goals and career-related goals.

Academic goals could mean the desire to get straight 'A's or even to plan to improve her grades i in the upcoming examinations. So if her long-term goal is to finish the school year with an A grade in every subject, her goal for the short term should be to put in an extra hour of work to her study time. Social and emotional skills are a large part of being a happy teenager. We all need these skills to build healthy relationships with other people, but in a phase when having peers and being liked means the whole world to them, your teen will need your assistance to develop healthy and realistic goals. According to the American Psychological Association (APA)'s booklet called *Developing Adolescents*, emotional intelligence involves both self-awareness and relationship building skills. Both these components are vital for the formation of quality relationships.

An example of a social and emotional goal would be your daughter's plan to stop talking behind a friend's back. Parents need to be alert because there can be unreasonable goals such as wanting to lose too much weight too soon in order to look good at a classmate's birthday party. Goals are not always rational when there is so much pressure to be "the popular girl."

Extracurricular goals are those that she must set to keep herself occupied with something other than schoolwork and socialising. In fact, the activities can be the route to a healthier body and slim appearance – something that every thirteen-year-old girl is striving to acquire. You can help her set goals even if she is shy and afraid that her peers will laugh at her inabilities.

Her goal could be to join the school debate team or craft club. Or she may choose to apply for the following year's drama competition. There are always different sports to choose from. If her school doesn't have all of them, she can be enrolled somewhere else near her house. Tennis and swimming are favourites. But check out your city's facilities for basketball, gymnastics and other sports. And if she wants to try an extracurricular activity that you believe is too rough for her, do not tell her that it isn't something that girls should do. Instead, let her try it out and see if it fits. And do remember that being involved in constructive activities keeps her busy and makes way for new friendships outside her classroom.

Vocational goals are rarely steady from thirteen to adulthood. One school semester she will be obsessed with drawing clothes and say that she wants to be a fashion designer, and then the next year she will ask you advice about becoming a lawyer. Watching successful women in TV shows and in movies, or reading about them, can make certain jobs seem quite appealing until the next one occupies her mind.

It's alright. She's only thirteen, so experimentation and finding out what her choices are is normal. Just make sure that she knows what her choices are because too many parents set early vocational goals for their teens, giving them misery later when they find themselves stuck in a career that has nothing to do with their aptitude and interests.

Think about the girl who was forced to become an engineer because her father would not love her otherwise. Then think about the girl who was told to take up a science subject because only then would people take her intelligence seriously. Why would you as a parent contribute so much, to her unhappiness?

When parents help their young teenager set goals, being realistic and to-the-point is key. Pleasing other people should not be the motivation behind any of her goals. It does not work most of the time. No goal should be made because a friend, crush, parent or sibling said that is what she must do. She needs to ask herself what she wants and share her thoughts with you. You can then help her write out her goals. Once a child makes a goal based on somebody else's desire, she may start out well but it is hard to stay on the path because her enthusiasm may last long for something that she did not want to do in the first place.

It won't be all smooth, of course. There will be obstacles along the way, but they are a part of the process as her brain continues to learn. She won't be able to reach every goal. She may not achieve a few goals and give up for a while, but that happens to everybody – even adults. She needs to know that she is doing fine and should not hate herself.

The fear of failure needs to be dealt with. A University of California professor- Martin Covington- stated that "the fear of failure is directly linked to your self-worth, or the belief that you are valuable as a person." His research has found that students generally fall into four categories when it comes to the subject of dealing with failure.

First, the Success-oriented students are the children who love learning for the sake of learning and see failure as a way to improve their ability, instead of a stain on their personal values.

The Second category on this list are come the Overachievers. These students avoid failure by putting in immense effort and succeeding. They are motivated by their fear of being proven imperfect human beings. These children can be heard telling their peers that they hardly spent time studying for an exam, when they really stayed up all night to prepare for it. This kind of behaviour is the result of an intense fear of failure and intense self- doubt.. It obviously acts as an ego boost when a girl does very well after she tells her classmates that she hardly studied.

The third group, the Failure-avoiding children, don't expect to succeed but they want to avoid failure. They believe that if they put in a lot of work but still fail, then this shows low ability and hence, low worth. On the other hand, if they don't try hard and still fail, this will not affect their value in their eyes. Children in this category are known to make excuses about assignments, delay, stay away from activities, and choose near-impossible tasks. In the end, the teacher who notices the lack of effort can punish them or they just fail.

The last category of children is called the Failure-accepting students. They are the ones who have stopped trying to succeed because repeated failed attempts have made them believe that they cannot do well. If they happen to perform well on a task, they will give the credit to anything but themselves., If your daughter is in this category, she would say that her test went well only because the questions were easy.

Parents and teachers play a big role in removing the fear of failure from a teenager's mind. The girls (and boys) who are motivated by the fear of failure are usually those whose parents rarely praise success but are quick to punish failure. When a girl believes that her parents will love her only if she does well, imagine the stress that is inadvertently induced by her parents.

Meher Pudumjee's Story

13

Most girls expect a lot from turning thirteen. So did I. My teens were accompanied by new expectations from everybody around me. Fortunately for me, my expectations were fulfilled. I had quite a liberal mom, so freedom, independence, parties, boys and music – I experienced it all, but in moderation.

Social life for today's Indian child is very different from that of my teen years. The world is so connected these days with Facebook, FaceTime, Twitter and blogs that you're just constantly in touch with friends and family across the globe. This also means that the influence that social media has on a youngster today is enormous and kids are very impressionable! The challenge is using these interactive tools for positive outcomes and not fall victim to negative effects.

Cyber bullies and fake identities infiltrate the web. Through peer pressure or otherwise, you are almost forced to share every detail of your life with thousands or millions of people online. Privacy is intruded upon. But that's how we adults feel about thirteen-year-olds today and not what the young ones believe! They think that widely open communication on the Internet is a normal part of life. We worry, but young boys and girls only see the entertaining side of socialising online. I see this with my own children!

When I was about fifteen, my dad underwent a heart bypass surgery in London. A day after the surgery, he suffered a stroke and could not speak or even recognise anyone. Suddenly, words and numbers made no sense to him. As his world turned topsy-turvy, my mom bore the brunt of it all. I watched them cope with the ordeal and felt admiration for them. My mom was the epitome of patience and a pillar of support for my dad. My dad's tenacity and focus on getting well was inspiring.

When he was frustrated because he couldn't tie his own shoelaces since he had lost the ability to grip anything with his fist, his physiotherapist helped him conquer the temporary disability. He asked him to be patient for a month and tie a bow on his thigh for the period. My dad practiced all night and the next morning - he was able to tie his own shoelaces. He worked hard to get back to his old self, practicing writing pages and pages of the alphabet and numbers, until he was able to return to almost normal life.

He had such perseverance that even after that stroke, he continued to head our family business and eventually wrote his book. This entire experience resulted in many lessons for me. The learnings are still a part of my life in both explicit and implicit ways. Sometimes, I do not even realise that those same learnings are being used in my own actions.

My dad taught me another important lesson when he came to spend three days with me during a break. I used to play the piano and was taking part in a competition at my school in the UK at that point of time. He hired a room with a piano so that I could practice. I had to repeat various parts of the Moonlight Sonata until each section was perfect. I was grateful for the initiative he took to help me perform well. I remember his words to me, a few minutes before the concert began: "Darling, now play to express rather than impress".

These words have become deeply ingrained in me, in every aspect of my life.

Along with my dad, my mom has been a solid support for me throughout my childhood and adult years. She believed in the philosophy of helping me reach my own decisions, whether right or wrong. As I was growing up, I had boyfriends, which was anathema to my dad, but meant a lot to me at that age.

It was my mother who helped my father deal with his own anxiety, rather than dumping the stress onto me. She would always sit down with me and help me rationalise the pros and cons of any situation. Then she'd leave it up to me to decide what I thought was best. Mom is a social worker by training and has always been involved with social projects, whether it was bringing home two child beggars from the street and hoping to bring them up to our home, or working with women and children to better their lives. This has had a profound impact on me, not so much as a child, but in my grown up years. Seeing her dedication and passion, I feel a strong desire to devote some of my time and effort to those less privileged than me.

With regard to education, like most Indian students, my last two years of school were spent going from one tuition class to the other. I had no time for sports, music or anything that was non academic. Indeed, I was satisfied with my life and found that playing my piano, or meeting my friends at tuitions were good stress busters. I guess we all adjust to our routines. When it came to priorities at school, I did not have any specific goals. Basically, I aimed to give of my best and try and do well in whatever I took on. Then as it happens with any young girl, I started dreaming about my future career. When I was 9 or 10 years old, my heart was set on becoming an air hostess. But as I moved on to my teenage years, that dream changed - I wanted to become an entrepreneur and open coffee shops.

Along with my goals, my interests also took a turn. I was about twelve or thirteen when I started enjoying the Sciences. This change could be credited to my science teacher who was fabulous – so much depends on a good teacher! But I still did not have a precise goal to become an engineer or join the family business. At that time, I was too preoccupied with my focus on learning many things at once and being a good student overall. My piano teacher thought I had the talent to become a concert pianist some day. That was not meant to happen because I had no such desire. I played the piano purely for relaxation.

It was while doing my junior college that I felt more confident in my academic preferences and chose to study engineering. My parents always maintained that my brother and I should take subjects that we enjoy, since that would bring out the best in us. Did they push us to have big, hairy, audacious goals – no, they did not. But what they did do is to push us to give of our best in whatever we chose to do. They used this approach whether it was the piano, an elocution competition or academics.

In India, with the massive gap between supply of good, affordable schools and colleges, and demand for education, there is severe competition as also social pressure to do well; thanks to which we cannot afford to mess up – most kids have that one chance to get into a good educational institution. This is probably the reason we take failure or a slip in our grades badly.

We have all gone through challenging and difficult times as we grew up, but what helps is an honest, transparent, open relationship with your kids – one in which they feel ok to confide, to tell the truth. Communication is paramount.

Parents need to help their teenage kids to be caring, confident young adults with a positive attitude to life.

Depending on priorities, circumstances and the opportunity of choice, I think it's vital to take up what you enjoy most. I have an eighteen-year-old son who was always good at Math and Physics. He loved to solve problems, taking it as an enjoyable challenge of sorts. When he completed his tenth grade, we encouraged him to take an aptitude test just so that he could gauge his strengths. This was very helpful, because it led him to decide to take on the Sciences and then aim for engineering as his profession.

On the other hand, my daughter who is fifteen was never really drawn to Math and Science when she studied in India, but in Singapore, she is doing well and is now enjoying Math and Biology. Once again, so much depends on the teacher. A good teacher can make or break a kid's aspirations and love for a subject. While my daughter is still not sure about what she plans to do after she finishes school, she has enormous confidence in herself, which will help her figure her career out.

Compared to the days when we were growing up, wherein choices for careers were limited to being an engineer, doctor or a chartered accountant, today there are so many options.

Goals are not associated with studies and careers only. As parents, my husband and I believe in a well-rounded education; having said that, we did choose a school known for its academics. However, we encouraged both our children to play a musical instrument, which they started at age 8 and have been playing ever since. Music is a huge stress buster – when they feel down and out or upset, I often see them at the guitar, piano or drums. In addition to music, both of them are interested in sport and have been part of their school basketball teams – a blend of exercise, lessons in teamwork, confidence, and recreation – all extremely important.

I also firmly believe that stopping an extracurricular activity when grades go down isn't always the right decision. Goals do not have to be in conflict with each other. They can exist independently and not affect each other. I say this because when my daughter's marks slipped in the eighth standard, we stopped her basketball, which in hindsight was very wrong on our part. Discussing the problem with her would certainly have been a wiser step.

I guess parenting is not always easy – we have made and continue to make mistakes, but hopefully with each mistake, we learn a lot and become that much wiser!

Chapter 5

The First Crush

Every girl in her early teens is going to have a crush. As hormonal activity goes up and the body starts to change, her interest in the opposite sex is going to increase. Coupled with the peer pressure to be liked, a girl's first crush is a serious part of growing up. Some families don't like the idea of their little girl spending her time and emotions on a boy when school work should be prioritised. You cannot really blame them because thoughts of the crush can take up study time and affect her performance.

If parents are logical, they will accept that the first crush – and more crushes – is part of every teen girl's life. The objective should be to remain open to communication so that your daughter doesn't hide her crush or, at a later stage, her boyfriend from you. Phone conversations you eavesdropped on, or from scribbles of the boy's name all over her notebook, is not the best way to find out.

It means that your child is too scared to share her emotions and life outside home with you. This can be dangerous if she actually begins to date a boy and wants to become physically involved or even ends up going somewhere without telling you, and they subsequently get into trouble.

Parents, your daughter will have that exciting first crush, regardless of your attempts to stop her. You could put her in an all girls' school and still see her falling for a boy at an inter-school event, in the neighbourhood or somewhere else. If you tell her to stop talking to boys, that would be unhealthy. There is no reason why she should think that boys and girls are not supposed to interact with one another. In fact, in some cases this kind of severe restriction makes the teen more curious about what she is missing. That can lead to trouble as well.

If she mentions your crush to you and defines it as 'love', don't tell her that it is nothing serious. Your daughter is as serious about her first crush as you were about marrying your husband. That is how important this is to her. And if she is being open about her feelings for a boy, you can be assured that she probably won't hide anything from you. She can meet him at the mall with other friends, knowing that you her parent and -support system, is alright with her hanging out with her crush.

She can even imbibe lessons from you about self-respect. When a boy she likes is disrespectful to her, she should know that she doesn't deserve that. For example, if her first crush doesn't share her feelings, he could be mean to her in front of their classmates. That would break her heart but she needs to know from you that the boy's behaviour was bad and it had nothing to do with her. Parents play a significant role in helping their daughters repair their broken confidence. The teen years are famous for ups and downs in confidence, and the first crush often contributes to a lot of it. Be happy if she comes to cry to you. That means that she trusts you and isn't hiding her social life from you.

Then, there are the crushes on celebrities which can range from collecting posters of the person to performing rituals in front of his picture every day. Cricketers, singers, actors and anybody else who fits her current idea of the ideal man could all be her potential first crush If your daughter's first crush falls under this category, you can worry a little less and step in to speak to her only if the crush is affecting her grades or causing irrational behaviour. Think about a girl who stops eating because her crush gets married. That is obviously taking things too far. So do watch out for unhealthy addiction!

As she grows older, your daughter may have a boyfriend. Steady relationships that last through the teen years are common. Then there are the on and off relationships where they are dating and not dating and then dating again. Of course there are those teenagers who consider a 'date' to be a meeting at a coffee shop or a movie. Your daughter may go on dates with one boy in class and then break up with him the next month and have a new boyfriend, or she may stick to the same relationship for a long time.

Depending on your family's traditions and values, you could make it clear to your child that dating won't be permitted until they reach a certain age. Or if the case is that dating is not allowed at all, she needs to be told before it is too late. The challenge is to be an understanding parent who she won't hide her crushes or boyfriends from. Meeting a boy in secret can mean trouble in the future if she is not given clear guidelines about age appropriate behaviour. Shying away from the topic of sexual activity and its consequences is not a good idea.

And girls, you can have fun but be responsible too. You will feel strange when you're around your first crush – and the following crushes – but shyness and warm feelings are what most people experience. You will want to talk to him on the phone, meet him outside school and even have thoughts of spending the rest of your life with him. Just remember that nobody has the right to make you feel bad or ask you to do something that you are not comfortable doing. Of course, remember that your parents were your age once and had crushes too, so you can always talk to them.

Admittedly, with the first crush can come the pain of the first heartbreak, and that can be difficult to deal with. When your daughter's first crush feels the same way about her, she will be ecstatic and float around on an invisible cloud. But if the boy doesn't like her at all or makes it a point to show his dislike, she will need time to get over the suffering. Parents and older siblings can share their own experiences and let her know that the heart will mend itself soon. The same goes for the girls who are rejecting the boys who have a big crush on them; don't be mean. Don't say something that will make him feel like he isn't good looking enough or nice enough. Just say you don't feel that way about him.

According to BBC UK, researchers have identified pathways in the brain which light up when teenagers are in love. They have compared the phenomenon of teenagers falling in love to the effect that cocaine has on the brain. That is how pleasurable the feeling of love is for your daughter. It's like an addiction. An addiction needs serious attention. So being communicative is necessary here because don't forget that along with the deep emotions comes a rise in physical desire, which can lead to irresponsible behaviour.

Talk and share with each other.

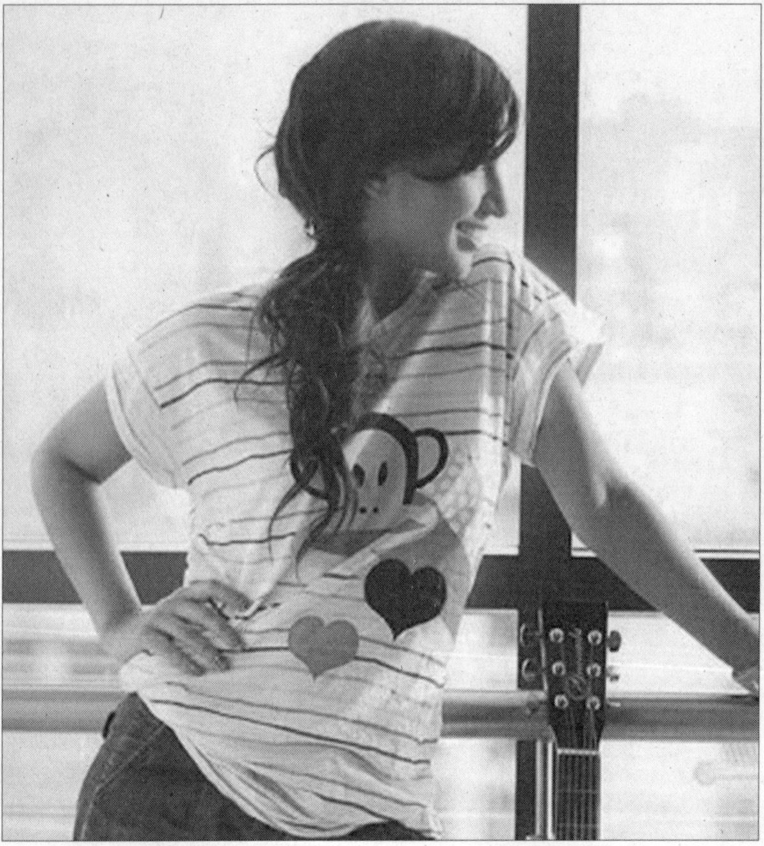

Malini Agarwal's Story

13

I don't think I had any major expectations from myself at age thirteen.

My life was already quite eventful and interesting because my father was a diplomat. This meant that I spent my childhood moving from place to place every three years. Starting from when I was six months old, I had already lived in India, Somalia, Lebanon, Germany and Greece by the time I hit my teens! In fact, when I was thirteen, my family and I came back to live in India for a few years. During that time, I went to Modern School on Barakhamba Road in Delhi. I remember watching the Republic Day parade with awe. I also have fond memories of hanging out with my friend in the Indian Foreign Service (IFS) colony, where we lived and we'd play for hours.

Life was simple and easy.

When I look at teens today, I realise that life was a lot less complicated back then. Peer pressure in terms of money, gadgets and brands didn't really exist when I was thirteen. I didn't have a cell phone at that age, nobody did. But most kids these days own an iPad, laptop and smartphone by the time they are thirteen (or even earlier)! When I was a kid we used the landline and had phone privileges that usually involved a cut-off time to receive calls. Walking around toting expensive toys was not really as common.

These days unfortunately there is an unhealthy focus on what kids own. That also makes things tough for the parents. And it's not always about what a family can afford. Sometimes it's a matter of deciding what a thirteen-year-old girl should be doing in her spare time. Also my folks were pretty adamant about teaching young me the value of money. Which, looking back I can appreciate. My mother taught me how to distinguish between my needs and my wants. But today it's much more complicated, "My friend X just got her own cell phone. Why can't I have one?" How do you compete with that?

Looking back, I also realise I had very little pressure to look a certain way or dress "fashionably". As the last of four kids I wore a lot of polka-dotted hand-me-downs which would make me a major fashion victim, even as a child, today! Today's 13-year-olds are very conscious of their appearance and the brands they are wearing. Grooming routines also begin early these days. In my time (and I cringe at how old I sound!) girls wouldn't start wearing makeup or threading their eyebrows till they were in their late teens! I don't think I even wore nail polish till I was 13!

Now-a-days with new malls sprouting everywhere and all this mega globalisation there are a crazy amount of choices and of course girls, influenced by marketing media all want to own the latest and look their best. In fact some of the most successful beauty bloggers are 13 or 14 years old!

When I was growing up, my friends and I would actually go play outside. We would arrange to meet each day after school in the garden below our building and have a great time playing hide and seek for hours. I suspect that game might be a little obselete today in the face of PS4! I remember vividly, being obsessed with these toys called the Glo Friends. They were little glow-in-the-dark snails and other creatures that would light up if you held them up next to a light bulb for a minute. I thought they were fabulous! So that's how we had fun; playing tag, running around without a care in the world or a single "Facebook Friend" .Unlike most of today's teenagers, I wasn't hooked onto technology, I barely even watched TV!

But yeah, my friends were definitely a big part of my life. I learnt a lot about friendship when I was thirteen. I even had my first 'boyfriend'. He was a boy named Arun who used to live in the same IFS colony. It was nice to have a boyfriend and feel special in that way for the first time.. And there was very little to stress about what other people thought of us, because nobody could comment on our pictures, since the ones we took would be on an old-school camera with film and 27 or 36 shots that we used sparingly on special occasions like birthdays.

Crushes were another exciting part of growing up. I remember my first crush. I was nine. My crush was a boy called Joel in my class in the 3rd grade in Athens, Greece. Joel made me feel all gooey inside and I could spend hours just staring at him. The way he looked, the way he played soccer with the other boys, the way he smiled – it's all so clear in my memory so obviously he made quite an impression. He definitely liked me back, but just like boys always do, he made a joke about how girls are gross and bounded away. In fact, most of my girlfriends were busy with their own crushes too, so we had fun bonding over that topic! I remember our sleepovers where we'd gush and giggle, about the boys we liked. Jumping around in PJs, playing board games and making blank calls to one of our crushes if we could sneak the phone (cord and all) into my room.

Although I was probably too young to understand those short-lived feelings, over the years I have come to recognise that familiar, self-conscious feeling as being a signal that I'm probably crushing on someone. You know that feeling where your life revolves around somebody else? When they become your reason to wake up in the morning? And you constantly daydream about them?

Luckily, my family has always been quite open-minded, so my crushes weren't a problem for them. They encouraged me to do a lot of extracurricular activities, I was allowed to go to school dances and be friends with boys. I took part in most things from dance to art to drama, and my mother would always be in the front row with a video camera! Filming all my special moments. Also, it probably didn't hurt that I was an honour roll student. Classic Indian nerd syndrome!

I know I've been going on about how great a crush can be, but crushes can also be devastating. Crushes can give you a reason to wake up and jump out of bed in the morning when you're thirteen. On the other hand, if the love is not reciprocated it can put you in a real funk. I remember being in love with a boy called Jose Olsen in the ninth grade. But he was in love with a French girl who had the same birthday as me. It was awful. Sometimes you know that the person you like already loves somebody else, but you can't help yourself! It's all part of growing up and it makes you who you are.

So, on that note I would say, love with reckless abandon, laugh out loud and dance like nobody's watching! After all, "the greatest thing you'll ever learn is just to love and be loved in return." Thank you, Moulin Rouge for that life lesson!

While being thirteen has its share of love, euphoria, infatuation and heartbreak, try to keep one eye on your goals. I know that when you like someone SO much, it's hard to focus on anything else. That's natural. Just remember that a thirteen-year-old's life should be made up of many wonderful people and experiences, and time and distraction are the best healers.

And now of course there's the challenge of managing relationships in the virtual space. With the Internet being so accessible and social media & technology like Facebook, Twitter, Instagram, Snapchat and Whatsapp, taking over our lives, today's thirteen-year-old girl needs to have some boundaries. Also recognise the difference between friendly banter and bullies. (Internet trolls are people who love to post off topic comments, evoke reactions from people by saying mean or nasty things. Your best revenge is to ignore them. And luckily most social media comes with a report abuse or ignore button, use it!

On a more serious note, people with bad intentions often come up with fake virtual personalities that lure young girls who are on the lookout for some kind of affection or popularity. This is called "Catfishing" A Catfish is someone who masquerades as another person and assumes a fake identity to initiate an often romantic relationship online. Girls this age can be extremely vulnerable to cyber harassment. Parents really need to keep an eye on this social media usage and monitor what their children are accessing.

Cyber bullying is a very real thing and girls need to have enough self-confidence to see them through all the experiences, good and bad, that they are bound to face. Imagine the plight of a young girl with low self-esteem, perhaps because she isn't popular at school or her crush is mean to her. A girl in her situation could be easy prey. And it isn't just about confidence building at school, parents need to provide a firm support system and reality checks and not sway to either extreme by becoming a scary adult who can't be confided in, or just a pal who lets their child, boy or girl, do anything they want at an age when they may not be equipped to handle the consequences. Or even understand what's happening.

I would say encourage your girls to share their feelings with you and create a positive loving environment of trust. Sometimes an older sibling can provide this support really well too! There is nothing wrong with having a crush, it's how we are programmed, and the less they have to hide, the safer they will be. It is also important that parents encourage a great deal of self-confidence and self-worth in their sons and daughters so that they can handle rejection when it happens, because it will. And it can be a great learning tool if approached correctly.

Every girl needs to know that the world isn't going to end when the boy she likes doesn't feel the same way about her. And she doesn't need to go looking for immediate validation in cyber space, somewhere where danger may be lurking. If her crush likes another girl in her class, that doesn't mean she is not good enough. It just means this boy was not meant to be a part of her life in that significant a way! And she needs to know this. And of course, parents need to be there, ever supportive and able to explain these new emotions to her as she feels them. In fact, sharing your own childhood experiences, crushes, excitement, failures and accomplishments is an excellent way to start. Good luck.

Pretty soon she'll be 13 going on 30!

Chapter 6

Friendship & Cliques

Friendship is an important F-word in a thirteen-year-old's life. The number of friends she has shows how much her peers like her. The kind of people she hangs out with determines her place in teen society. Is it with the popular girls or the uncool girls or is she a loner? Gone are the days where a girl would meet her friends at school and then at the park or at tuitions. Now they meet at those places and online too. What was restricted to the occasional phone call has become hours of chats on the Internet or mobile phone.

Text messaging, Whatsapp and Facebook make friendship easier to maintain and pave the way for new friendships. There are even communities for people who like or dislike the same thing. Bonding has never been the same before. As with everything, the negative has accompanied the positive and classmates and the entire social circle can see friends fighting and also putting an end to their relationship. The horrors of social media come to light with teenagers in different countries having committed suicide over such public insults.

There is still good news. *The Monitor*, a publication of the American Psychological Association, published an article in which a psychologist admitted that while technologies have changed the way teens interact, but today's young people still value the friends who they meet every day as their closest. Other psychologists, however, are concerned that the new modes of communication may affect a teen's social development. "The loss of [a] human voice", is something one psychologist is worried about. Parents of teenagers will identify with this opinion when they reflect on their own childhood where they weren't constantly typing and editing texts on their phones for the purpose of befriending people.

Research has consistently shown that teenagers without friends can suffer from long-term consequences including issues with social and moral development and cognition. *The School Psychology Review* (USA) once published the results of a study that concluded that friendless adolescents are more likely to be unemployed, aggressive or have poor mental health as adults. In non psychology language; this means that if your daughter is shy or unable to form friendships in person, she can use social media to build a social life from the security of her home.

A 2010 study by researchers at the Queensland University of Technology in Australia, found that lonely children and teens used the Internet to make new friends and even use the online medium to discuss personal and intimate subjects – more often than the participants who did not report loneliness at all. One of the co-authors of the research study explains that Facebook allows a user to create a brand new version of herself or himself – unlike a mirror which hides nothing. You can be a cool girl online or even a talkative girl, no matter what you are like with the people around you every day.'

With all the good and bad observations about online

and mobile socialising, it is good practice for parents to encourage their daughters to meet friends in the same physical environment. She can spend time actually speaking to her friends in social settings like cafes and restaurants. Or you can encourage her to resort to some good old fashioned socialising by visiting her friend's houses after school or on weekends.You could organise small gatherings for her where she and her friends occupy themselves with games like Chinese whispers or board games such as Snakes and Ladders.

While you are monitoring your thirteen-year-old's relationships with her friends and Best Friend Forever (BFF), don't be surprised to realise that she is a member of a clique. A clique is a small group of people who are very close to each other and are reluctant to let others join them. Cliques typically consist of a few girls who talk alike, have the same interests, dress alike and spend all their time together.

Basically, they socialise only within their own clique. All the other girls are outsiders. The concept of a clique can sound unhealthy at times, but they are prevalent in teenage life. Plus, they are not always bad. Some girls form supportive friendships with other clique members, creating a connection that lasts even when they are adults. And not all cliques go out of their way to make their peers feel unwanted.

There is a movie that could be called a psychology study about teenage cliques. Released in 2004, Mean Girls, starring Lindsay Lohan, gives an apt picture of the workings of a clique. In the movie, Cady is a sixteen-year-old girl who has just returned to the United States after twelve years spent in Africa with her parents who are zoologists. She has been homeschooled for all these years but is enrolled in a public school now. It starts with some classmates warning her about the school clique referred to as the Plastics.

Then the head of the clique, a girl called Regina, starts talking to Cady. This makes another girl unhappy because she sees Cady's success in almost becoming a clique member. What begins as a plot to get even with Regina and is motivated by jealousy, brings havoc into Cady's life. She tries to start a relationship with Regina's ex boyfriend, turns the other clique members against her and in the process, doesn't realise that she has become a second version of Regina herself. The way she dresses, the spiteful nature, and superficial behaviour all resemble Regina's.

One weekend when her parents are out of town, Cady hosts a party at their house. During the party, Cady ends up telling her boyfriend that she was failing math on purpose just so that he would talk to her. The boy is not happy to hear this and tells her that she is as bad as Regina. To make a long story short; Cady learns the hard way how cliques can ruin a girl's life and she gets back to her usual self at the end of the movie.

A teenager can easily fall prey to the copycat syndrome and the popular girls are not always popular for good reasons. Mean Girls displayed that. Parents can guide their daughters to maintain their individuality even as members of a clique. She needs to understand that enjoying time spent together during lunch recess or at each other's houses, doesn't imply that all the girls have to think the same and do the same or have the same physical appearance. And being a member of a clique also doesn't mean that you should shut out everybody else. Friendships can be found in different places.

Photo: Surinder Nagar

Suhasini Haidar's Story

13 When I was growing up, I was absolutely sure of two things when it came to birthdays. One was that I would learn to whistle when I turned eight. The other was that when I would turn thirteen, I would have that 'magic swan' moment. I'm talking about that instant when somebody turns into a beautiful and sophisticated person. I especially needed this to happen because I was all thumbs and two left feet.

Basically, if I walked, I would trip. When I ran, I often stumbled. So I was just an uncoordinated disaster. Still, there was the time when I felt that I may make a mark in gymnastics. My coach even groomed me for an inter-school competition, but when I saw all the other contestants pirouetting with such grace, I faked a stomach ache to escape ridicule. Just like all other childhoods, mine was full of bottled up fears that seemed laughable later on in life.

The bad news was that becoming a teenager didn't change things. The good news was that being awkward didn't matter that much to me anymore. The more confident me still wasn't any good at sports, but I took to public speaking and writing. Even if I didn't have a magic swan moment, I felt better about this change. Oh, and I never learned to whistle either.

Looking back at my life then and comparing it with the

daily lives of my two daughters, I believe that young girls today miss the ability to travel around the city on their own. When I was thirteen, I would cycle to school, take public buses to my friends' houses and walk to most places. In fact, my friends and I couldn't afford scooter-rickshaws or taxis most of the time, but we were happy to cram into one and go to a movie or go on a shopping trip.

We managed our own money. If we ran out, we just had to deal with it by borrowing or walking the long way home. In contrast, my daughters never go anywhere unescorted and they wouldn't dream of taking their cycles outside our colony. When I ask them if they need pocket money, they ask me, "For what?"And while my parents had only a vague idea of where I would be when I was out, as long as I was home by a certain time, I know down to the nearest GPS location, where my daughters are at all times. Thanks to mobile phones.

The truth is that we have traded in all that freedom for our daughters' safety and security. Admittedly, some of the most unpleasant moments of my teenage years involved groping hands, lewd comments and the suggestive winks of men in public places and on DTC buses.

Now I shudder at what my daughters would do, never having been exposed to dangers in the way we were. Of course, the dangers are countless. I want our girls to know that molestation, rape, and violence are not necessarily things that happen to other people. They can happen to anybody. From the moment that a child becomes a teenager and starts to menstruate, adults begin to worry about well-being in a different way than before. There is concern that you will be attacked sexually and scarred for life. The important thing is to know that it is not your fault if you were alone in a situation with your attacker. It's not your fault if someone took advantage of you. And nobody has the right to judge you.

When I think about all this, I remember meeting a former beauty queen once who had an amazing story. Linor Abargil was a model and Miss Israel when a man she knew raped her at knifepoint. She told me that when she called her mother to tell her what had happened, her mother simply said: "Get to safety and tell me where you are. And don't take a shower until the police examine you." At that moment, she said that if her mother had said anything else, or asked her why she had been with the man in the first case, she would have collapsed. But her mother's non-judgmental words told her that it wasn't her fault. This changed the way that she looked at her ordeal. Two months later, Linor went on to win the Miss World title. Today, she is a successful lawyer in Israel.

Besides being exposed to challenges regarding safety, thirteen was an important age for me when it came to academics. Until then, I had been easy going about my grades, but now I began to take my studies seriously. I did this for myself and not because my parents or teachers had told me to. With time, I realised that if you enjoy what you do, it doesn't seem like hard work anymore. I guess that guides me today too. Sometimes it isn't for the best. For instance, there are times that I find it hard to accept assignments that I don't enjoy. But the advantage of this habit makes any work that I enjoy doing, end up done quite well. If I like what I am doing, I give it my all. Even sleeping and eating become unimportant.

At that age, I also learned that there are no short cuts; the road to excelling at school or in extracurricular activities is always through disciplined and focused hard work. You will meet a lot of people who say that they do things instinctively and that they never need to study but 'somehow' manage to do well. Know that they are either lying or are the exception.

Another lesson that I was taught during my thirteenth

year was the importance of making new friends while never giving up on old friendships. I remember when I was going into the 9th Grade, the school split me and my best friends into different sections. I was upset with my teachers because I felt cheated of time with my friends. It took me a while to talk to the kids in my own section. I guess I did that partly in defiance of the school's decision. Instead, I would spend every spare moment trying to figure out how to meet my best friends. Soon, I gave in to my situation and made many new friends at school. When you are that young, you think that every decision made by grown-ups is just a way of controlling you, so you try to fight it.

Along with the lesson in making new friends, I learned my first lessons of the heart - a first crush and a first break-up. I learned that it's better to say no right away and risk losing a friendship than hurting someone's feelings. Every girl needs to value her own feelings and be aware that nobody's heart breaks forever. It is also a fact that nothing, absolutely nothing, is the end of the world.

At thirteen, friendships are everything. I had three best friends. We were a part of a gang of ten girls. Just like any girl of that age, I was more likely to listen to my friends than anybody else in the world. As I grew older, I realised how important it was to have that support system in place. My confidence to deal with anything was the result of knowing that my best friends would be there for me no matter how badly I messed up. In turn, I learned to return that loyalty.

Life in a teen's world may be largely the same these days, but today's teenagers don't need much advice. After meeting lots of kids in their early teenage years, I am amazed by their strength and confidence. Most of them have never known that gawky, awkward stage that I had. Still, I would tell any young girl that your obvious assets including good looks, great hair and super grades are all gifts that you should be proud of. But eventually, it is our weaknesses, or our differences from others, that will make us who we are. In my own case, I believe that because I wasn't that good at the Sciences, I ended up discovering what I could do well. It was because I was shy that I made an effort to get to know other shy people. Also, my fear of being a social outcast made me sensitive to the feelings of other people who got picked on.

In the world of media where I work, I quickly understood that perfection isn't all that perfect, that it's the quirks of people that make them effective communicators. You'll notice that most popular TV show hosts have an obvious difference about them that appeals to viewers. Some of them are bald. Others are huge. Then there are the ones with strange accents. These are people who millions of people want to watch for hours. So remember that while everyone in school is trying to be that super-thin glamorous girl in a small black dress, it is the ones that stand out for other reasons that often steal the show!

Even with the Internet and social media taking over our lives, I don't see a major problem. These girls are younger than instant messaging and many social networking sites, so they have grown up in a world that has always blurred the lines between real and virtual socialising. The key is to make sure that thirteen-year-olds know that there is a difference between the real and the virtual. I would put it this way: Remember that all technology is a resource. Your cell phone or laptop is a tool for you to connect to others more effectively. Talk to your friends, share your homework assignment online, chat with a cousin who lives abroad, but learn to switch it off or turn away from it when you don't need to use it. It is a force multiplier - not a force that should control you.

I loved being a part of my ten-girl gang that hung out

together. At that age, there was a crazy rush to be seen as a clique member. It proved that you fit in. Some of our school mates would talk about us with admiration, others with envy. I do think it was a happy time for us in the clique, but despite all the common ground, we all soon grew up to do very different things. It was only later when I caught up with these same school friends, did I realise how everybody else saw our clique. Many of them saw us as elitist and aloof girls who were unwilling to mix with others. I am proud of my friendships from that age, and happy that we do still keep in touch, though not as a clique. Many of us now have children who are teenagers, or are getting there, and it is lovely to see that the cool clique has transformed into a network based on common ground that was built on a shared history of being so connected all those years ago.

There are some valuable points that I wish someone had told *me* at 13. Here goes:

Be you. Your friends, your family, your dogs and pets love you for who you are.

Friendship is a two-way street. Your friendships reflect you, and you will always get back whatever you put in.

You don't always feel like engaging. That's fine. But if you hurt someone who wants to reach out to you: a classmate, a grandparent, a friend, say sorry straight away.

Love, heartbreak, relationships are words that sound like they last a lifetime. They don't. Friendships and memories do.

Chapter 7

Staying Safe Offline & Online

There's hardly any place in the world that can be called safe. Everybody needs to be careful and do their best to stay out of danger. For the new teenager, safety is a big challenge because of her increasing independence. When she was younger, she would not go anywhere without you. Inside school was the only place where she would be without you.

If she met friends after school or during the weekends, they would be at each other's houses or at the mall with either of their parents. All that changes as she approaches her teens. Now she meets friends for movies and unsupervised trips at the mall. Her social life is heavily connected to the online world. You'll rarely see her make eye contact with you when her phone is in her hands. If you haven't given her a phone yet, she won't turn around from the computer most of the time.

With all the time spent on the Internet and the rest of the time outside with her friends, your child is at a high risk of violence and assault. The key is to make her aware, teach her how to respond if something happens. In other words, you need to make her ready to face all possibilities.

The attachment to digital technology is a phenomenon that previous generations will have trouble identifying with. Recent research indicates that social media including Facebook and Twitter are preferred over email – by people of all ages. The trouble with being so technologically savvy is that girls with hardly any maturity have access to everybody and everything, with too many people having access to them too.

The use of these devices needs to be monitored when she is this young. Nobody is telling you to steal her password and go into her account to see her online interactions. What you should do is keep a track of her social media usage habits. For instance, ask her who she has been chatting with on Facebook. You could ask her who she follows on Twitter. Try to keep the curious tone out of your voice because if she thinks you are suspicious about her friends, she won't share any information with you.

Another step that you can take to protect her from online predators is to change the location of your computer. Tablets and phones can definitely be moved around the place, but you can install your computer in a common area of the home. If she uses social media in the living room where you all spend your evenings, you can pass by and check on her activities. Plus, you can easily see how long she spends socialising online.

Tell her you are interested in seeing her profile. Let her know that she should not talk to strangers online, just as she shouldn't talk to strangers in the real world. Don't forget to remind her about cyber bullying. Show her the latest newspaper articles featuring girls who have committed suicide because their peers bullied them online. Your child needs to know that she can go to prison for being publicly mean or spreading rumours online.

If somebody is bothering her, show her how to use privacy settings to block the person or report abuse. It would be convenient to tell her to be your Facebook friend so that you can keep track of her social media behaviour and interactions. She could say she doesn't want to be connected to you online because she would rather have a private life away from your watchful eyes, but you must be firm.

Don't ignore addictive habits. Some girls may chat online more than others. You need to be alert so that your daughter doesn't overuse her privileges and make her studies or physical social life suffer. That means that she should not be spending all weekend or all evening stuck to the computer desk chair. Long SMS or Whatsapp chats very harmful if they are consuming all of her free time. If you think she is too attached to her mobile phone, ask her to show you who has been sending her SMSs lately. Check her phone log once in a while.

You can set a day to check her email too. Tell her why you are doing it. If you share your concerns with her, she may react less strongly to your decision. Consider setting time limits for both her Internet and phone use. Social media addiction needs to be kept at bay. Watch out for the signs; if she is losing sleep and meals because she is too occupied online, or not doing well in school because of over usage, she may be addicted and need psychological help.

All the evils are not all online. Girls, you need to be alert when you are outside the home. Keep your eyes on the road ahead of you when you are walking. Do not stare at your phone's screen while you type away. If you are listening to music on your portable music player, don't close your eyes and sing or hum. Eyes open always. Second rule for you; don't go out alone. Irrespective of age, there is safety in numbers. And never leave the house without telling your mother or father where you are going. If you think you are going somewhere that they won't approve of, don't lie and say you're somewhere else. Think about what would happen if you got into trouble outside and needed their help. Lying never brings good.

One more piece of advice for you, girls. If someone you know or a stranger touches you in a way that doesn't feel right, you have the right to tell him or her to stop it. For all you know, the person maybe trying to coerce you into being physically intimate with him. You must say no. If peers try to make you do something that you don't feel comfortable doing, say no.

Don't be bothered about what they will say about you 'chickening' out. What matters is that you are safe.

Anjali Sharma's Story

13

When I turned thirteen, I believed that a whole new world would open up for me. Thankfully, I was right. My teens were certainly a prelude to an exciting phase of life, followed by an exciting adulthood. As is the case with most young girls, I expected enhanced privileges, less monitoring and lots of privacy from my parents. I wanted to be more independent in every way. In a nutshell, I anticipated a new life where the grown-ups would not interfere. While my parents did start treating me like the adult I was on my way to be, they did not cease to monitor me. I appreciated the freedom and the monitoring turned out to be necessary. My parents were my constant source of support.

If I look back at those years, I see most of the challenges of being a teenage girl in India, or for that matter, anywhere else in the world, the same today as when I was growing up. Being a teen is accompanied by changes in the female body. There is a flush of what will follow. Every young girl has her share of experiences with males showing an obvious interest in her now. There will be boys and men who are anything but sensitive or decently behaved. These are the ones who will direct slang words at you and try to get close to you, making you uncomfortable about their presence.

Handling such situations is always a persistent challenge. With reduced privacy both online and offline today, there is so much more exposure. Girls can find themselves facing unwelcome interest from various channels. Social networking sites, mobile telephones and the like, make it easy for the opposite sex to systematically 'execute' this interest. Sending a message with a click or keeping track of her whereabouts or admiring her photographs, the internet makes all of this possible. It is for this reason that crimes against girls and women have risen.

Back then, we did not have the Internet. In fact, there was no such concept or none that I knew of in any case. Life comprised of simpler things. Children were used to more outdoor activity and much more reading. Now, however, there are lots of things to choose from. Children have books, ebooks, DVDs, mp3 players and more malls and restaurants around them. There are more ways to spend time with friends. There are too many things that lead a girl to find out about the good, bad and the ugly at an early age.

The Internet is a boon and a curse at the same time. On the one hand you are getting empowered by access to so much information, on the other hand you deal with the problems of greater infringement of privacy and cyber crime. Little girls need to be guided on what kind of personal information they should share on their online profiles because stalking is a real threat. Only responsible use can keep her safe.

There are indeed major safety concerns related to online socialising. Aside from the stalkers, there will be friend requests from people with bad intentions on social networking sites. Then there's hacking. One day you could find your email account or Facebook account hacked into and see messages in your Sent Items that you've never sent yourself.

Or you could find strange pictures uploaded onto your page,

making your friends online wonder about your suddenly odd behaviour. Changing your password periodically can help combat that. And don't tell anybody what your password is because teenagers can be vengeful and an angry friend won't hesitate to log on to your account and mess up your social life online. While there are laws in place to check all of this, the implementation is the issue. Parents need to be careful with their daughter's online activity since this is a time when she is an easy victim with all the attention she is craving. How about a stranger asking her to meet her for coffee when she is feeling low about her crush not liking her? Or a girl who is overweight and upset about not being popular, jumps at the opportunity to interact with a member of the opposite sex. Dangerous.

My advice to every girl facing bullies online, is that she must share every bit of the information, including her part in it if any, with her parents. Show them each message or SMS that the bully has sent you. Don't wait to tell them. If he or she makes you feel scared or unsafe even once, you should not stay quiet. The law enforcement authorities can step in after that, assisting you to lodge complaints and applying remedies to keep the bully away. Even with the potential hazards, the Internet is here to stay. Being prepared is the smart thing to do. It is every parent's duty to let their daughters know that the Internet can be a powerful tool for academics, social outreach and social interaction but it can also be a source of peril. Explain the privacy settings on websites to her. If you are on the same social networking site, you can monitor her activity too.

Outside the home, there are the risks of interacting with strangers, especially if your daughter is a friendly, open-minded child. In India, we have to be mindful of the fact (and convey to our children as well), that our society is not very open about sex and sexuality. There is a huge amount of repression, which often lets itself out in harmful ways. Talking about sex and puberty is considered a sin by many people even today. Even talking to boys can be taken as a dirty deed by certain older people. There is mystery and negativity around the topic. With that cultural attitude, we have to caution our young girls to be on their guard when they are talking to or even sitting near strangers.

When my daughter is out with her friends, my husband and I tell her to keep informing us of her location, through text messages, or Whatsapp messages. So there is an example of how so many devices and the information age help us. Both of us also keep her friends' numbers handy with us. We always have the numbers of the friends that she's out with, for establishing contact if the need arises. Time limits are also set by us. She is not allowed to remain outside after a certain hour. In my view, all of these measures are absolutely necessary. Parental monitoring at some level has to continue through her teens to ensure her safety. You have to work on establishing a boundary between guidance and dictatorship. Being open and honest is the key.

Communication is vital. I think that parents and children need to keep talking to each other and sharing with each other. In most cases, if parents don't come down too hard on their daughters and instead calmly explain their concerns to them, there is a smaller chance of them reacting as if you are ruining their lives. Explain the motivation behind your concerns because she can identify with the risks too. In fact, maintaining a constant dialogue with your teenager is the best weapon against the risks and challenges that surround her.

Chapter 8

Boys Vs. Girls

India has the dubious distinction of being a country known for its gender discrimination. Figures collected by economists may indicate progress in terms of a higher number of female CEOs and leading politicians, but the literacy rate still remains a disparity between girls and boys, women and men. The cruel practice of female infanticide and gender-selective abortion exists even with sex detection before birth being banned in this country.

A lot of Indians still see the boy child as superior. In some families, this attitude remains till the daughter is older, married and performing her duties as a wife and mother. Even with the changes around us in big Indian cities, there are girls suffering from discrimination in the rural areas and in their own houses within the city.

You don't need to look too far to feel the gender gap. When you turn on the television set, most of the daily TV serials emphasise the way many Indians expect their girls to behave. You see the older generation of women whose lives revolve around pleasing their husbands and taking care of their sons – until the sons are found equally dutiful wives. Then you see the younger generation come into the picture. If she wants to go out with her husband on a date or wears something that doesn't fit in with the traditional image – salwar kurtas or saris – she is considered a rebel, a misfit.

When a female protagonist wants to take her own decision regarding her pregnancy or even fighting for a girl she sees being harassed by men on the street, it appears that her in-laws and husband seem to think that they have the right to chastise her for thinking with her own mind. Then there are the female characters that start out as independent young women with careers and the ability to stand up for themselves. Sadly, they regress to meek, voiceless women, after the family elders and husbands point out their inappropriate behaviour.

After watching the women stand there and listen to so much so silently, viewers must wonder how a person in their right mind can tolerate so much harassment for merely being themselves and not even harming anybody. Even more interestingly, the ladies seldom speak out against the men's wrongdoings or ill-treatment. In recent interviews, some of these television actresses have said that the content of the serials are in conjunction with what the average viewer identifies with.

Thankfully, your daughters are much more likely to watch English television shows like *How I Met Your Mother* or *Breaking Bad*. The point is this; most of the Indian daily shows are not full of the best role models. In contrast, non Indian girls are shown to be more assertive, ambitious and have their own voice.

Those of you who are encouraging your thirteen-year-old daughter to think about college and law school or medical school or any other higher education plans, are fighting the statistics that plague India. The ratio of female to male enrollment in primary education is effectively equal, but in higher education, there is a wide gap with just over 40 per cent of Indian college students being girls. Education is necessary to change cultural norms that are responsible for putting boys at a higher place.

There was a disturbing report on parental investment in India in University of Bristol's publication *Research in Public Policy* in 2011. The researchers observed that Indian boys are more likely to be given vaccinations than Indian girls. They also found that the boys are more likely to be given vitamin supplements and be breastfed for a longer time. In fact, the quality of childcare appeared to be better for the baby boys including aspects such as supervision and physical care. Just this one report spells out how much discrimination there is between boys and girls in certain parts of the country and in many urban families too.

In one such region called the Banda District in Uttar Pradesh, a dedicated group of women decided to conquer the suffering and obstacles faced by their females. Hence, the Gulabi Gang was formed by Sampat Pal Devi. The Banda District is one of the poorest districts in India and marked by patriarchal norms, rigid caste divisions, domestic violence, dowry demands, child marriages and female illiteracy.

The gang is called 'Gulabi' or 'Pink' because the members all wear pink saris. While the movement started with the aim to punish the men in the community who oppressed girl and the women, and to combat domestic violence and husbands leaving their wives, now they do whatever they can for human rights in the area as well. The members ensure the proper distribution of food grains to the poor and the disbursement of pension to old widows who have no documentation to prove their age. With time, they have become involved in helping any human being who is being abused. This movement gives Indian girls hope in nation where girls are still judged for their 'proper' or 'improper' behaviour, outlook and clothes.

Girls, you need to know right now that you can do anything that boys do. You can play soccer, if that's what you want to do. You do not ever have to wear skirts if you don't like skirts. You can be an engineer or a number crunching genius too, if that's what makes you feel good and if that's what you like to do. If somebody tells you that you should not play cricket because it is a game for boys, do not bother spending a second thinking about what he said. Did you know that India has a successful team of female cricketers?

What if somebody tells you that girls aren't supposed to become astronauts? Google 'Kalpana Chawla'. She was from Karnal in India and the first Indian woman in space. She was also the first Indian-American astronaut. Study well now. Soon, you will know which subjects you love enough to study more as you grow up. The Sciences are not for boys only. And the Sciences are not for girls either. They are for everybody. It is up to you to choose. Girls can do anything, and be anyone that they choose to be.

Komal Sood's Story

13

When I was thirteen, life was innocent. Those growing years were 'childlike' just as they should have been. I had no benchmark or expectations about starting my teens, instead I just took things as they came. But I do have some special memories of times shared with my mother. She is a beautiful woman and was even more gorgeous in her youth. She was very particular about grooming and beauty and made sure that I followed all of her beauty tips and stayed well groomed.

Of course, being thirteen had its share of challenges. The real test was more to deal with the changes in my physical body and to combat the hormonal changes that were causing unrest and excitement at the same time. Early teens can always be associated with growing breasts, bras and other signs of puberty. Still, life was much simpler back then. We grew up with just one channel on TV.

Then one fine day, Doordarshan was joined by almost two hundred new channels from different parts of the world. With American series such as *Friends, Sex and the City and Desperate Housewives*, becoming the daily staple for the modern Indian teenager, the level of exposure increased drastically. The effect on the youth in big cities like Mumbai and New Delhi was bound to be strong, but think about the cultural response of thirteen-year-old girls living in other parts of the country.

There are girls brought up in a more conservative, traditional manner. Imagine a girl who is used to wearing her salwar kameez and dupatta, not allowed to interact with boys and spends her days doing school work and helping with house work, being exposed to a different world through the television set. I believe that the multicultural exposure that the media today gives teenagers is a great way to educate the young mind. In fact, watching sitcoms, documentaries and news shows that focus on cultures far away, encourages a thinking process with a mind that is not resistant to new information. It is a privilege to have the opportunity to learn so much about the global space.

When I was growing up, my parents were a major source of support. They listened to me patiently as I shared my dilemmas with them. They stood by me when I was frustrated and confused, guiding me with solutions on the way. I was not happy with the Indian system of education. I don't remember the teachers being anything more than robots who came in for a while and then disappeared.

My father was in the Indian Army, so I studied in many convent schools around the country. Then I attended boarding school at Sophia School in Ajmer and later, Sophia college in the same city. My school years included four years at the British International School in Cairo, Egypt when my father was stationed there as a diplomat. The teachers abroad were a welcome change in my life. They were so much more interactive and approachable than any of the teachers I had encountered in my schools in India. In fact, they actually took an interest in every student, including me.

My fashion designing education took place at National Institute of Fashion Technology (NIFT) in Kolkata. I followed that course with training in patternmaking and marketing skills at Central Saint Martins in London. I'm sharing my educational background to put an emphasis on how good teachers and educators can make a big difference in a girl's life.

I remember that when I was around thirteen years old, I travelled a lot. When my father left his post in Cairo for a new position in Udaipur in Rajasthan, I had to get used to many new people and customs. However beautiful the City of Lakes was, the switch to an unfamiliar educational system was difficult at first. And then there was the culture shock of sorts after living in a foreign country for so long. It took some months, but everything was accepted and settled soon. So, the most important lesson that I learnt when I was around thirteen was the lesson of adaptability. I had to teach myself how to deal with change. Or rather, my experiences taught me how to adapt to changing circumstances. Till date, my adaptable nature and open mind remain my biggest strengths. These traits of my personality guide me.

They say that change is the only constant in life, and it's true. Way back in the 1980s when I was a young teenager, India was a different India. It was more traditional and closed. When I say closed I think of the mood that pervaded through India then as a nation and not my personal experience. Basically, the India now is progressive, youthful and more expensive. Back then, people did not travel as much on an international level. These days, making trips abroad for work and pleasure is common. It is as if Indian people in those days had an inferiority complex about themselves. Staying safely in their own cities and in familiar territory was the preference. Ten years ago, all that suddenly changed as trade and commerce policies brought on economic growth.

The media, education facilities, big brands – it's all here

now. Thus, people are travelling and experiencing much more in terms of what they are buying, seeing and learning. My travels have always enriched my life, so I believe that all this has been a great transformation. Thanks to my travels, I have always had a curious mind with brilliant powers of observation. The skills came from interacting with people who spoke differently, dressed differently and behaved unlike people in my own country or city. Even the fact that people in two countries do not look the same, taught me to appreciate all cultural differences. Yes, the thirteen-year-old girl should take every chance to visit unknown destinations.

As India has grown up, its citizens' aspirations have changed too. I notice that everybody wants more. They want more success in their education and careers. They also want to own more things. I believe that when all that is earned through the dint of hard work and dedication, that is positive. And it is both men and women who want much more. With the social changes taking place, even society's attitude towards girls has improved (in urban India at least). I see it as a natural progression with the country getting better at multiple things.

There are now fathers who want their daughters to be professionally skilled and climbing up the corporate ladder. There are women at the top ranks of many offices and they in turn empower girls who are trying to figure out what they will do when thcy grow up. Therefore, I see closer equality between girls and boys today.

When I was a teenager, I recall facing instances where adults tried to point out that boys are supposed to do certain things but girls should not try those things. Apparently, there were special rules for boys. Then there are the people who follow the ancient practice of labeling the boy child as a superior being. Unfortunately, India is known to be unsafe for girl and women, so I did feel the need to be protected. My army child situation enveloped me in culture, respect, sports, travel and protection. Girls do need to be careful about their well being even if they are able to do what boys can do at school, work or the playground.

Girls, my advice for dealing with adults who believe that girls should be treated as a weaker sex, is to explain to them that we, the female species, are natural multitaskers. We can be tomboys and play soccer during the day, and then dress up and be beautiful in the night at a social event. Don't compare yourself to boys or to other girls either. Do not fall victim to the harmful attitude towards boys and girls that some members of society have. Remember that the journey from a boy to a man is a more difficult one at times because society expects a boy to take on a competitive career option and be the head of a family.

In case of girls, that is still an option but not compulsory in many families. So, don't be angry at the boys when some grown up tries to belittle your gender. I think that the adults who have such opinions and judge little girls about their behaviour, should now be relics of the past. India is a young nation with 70 per cent of the population under thirty years old. Abundant growth has created job opportunities for both girls and boys. The days of choosing between engineer and doctor are gone. Careers that were considered unconventional in my childhood are now popular. Depriving girls of education, work opportunities and social importance, is like amputating the limbs of the nation.

Chapter 9

Everybody Wants to be Size 0

Why don't I look like the other girls? That is a common complaint that parents of teenage girls have to hear. You would think that your intelligent child would understand and appreciate that no two people look the same, but no. At age thirteen and going up the years, girls often struggle with their body image. 'Body image' is basically what she thinks of her body and how she feels about her body. The bad part is that this image of her body in her mind doesn't always match her body's real shape and size.

A teen with a positive body image has healthy thoughts about her body and accepts the way she looks, no matter how chubby or how thin she is. If she is unhappy with her body, she has negative body image. Since body image affects her confidence and lifestyle choices, helping her develop a healthy body image is vital. Think about it this way; if your daughter believes that she is 'too fat' and needs to lose weight immediately, she can resort to dangerous measures like starting a diet of only juice or giving up everything edible and drinking only water until she falls ill.

It isn't just the possibility of physical harm because when a girl is dissatisfied with the way she looks, it will ruin her social life too. It is not uncommon for negative body image to lead to eating disorders such as anorexia nervosa and bulimia. Anorexia results from starving herself, while bulimia involves vomiting out any food that she eats. So watch out for such behaviour and intervene before it gets out of control. Psychologists and psychiatrists, along with a dietician, can be of great help.

Multiple factors influence a girl's body image. Family environment is one. If somebody in the family constantly talks about her being too fat (an older sibling, for example) or frequently calls her fat, the child could easily start disliking her body even more than she already did and become focused on her so called ugly body. Skin colour affects body image too. Your daughter may hate her dark face and body. Nobody can deny India's weakness for light, nearly white complexions. There's the successful fairness products' market to prove it. But then we have celebrities like Nandita Das who show our girls that dark or light, any girl is beautiful and talented. Parents need to be like her. Encourage her to take care of her skin so that it is glowing and smooth regardless of its shade.

Then there is an entire industry that is frequently blamed for giving girls and women unhealthy ideals of body weight: the advertising and film industry. Those pictures in newspapers and magazines and those images in TV advertisements make girls wonder why they don't have those legs or that stomach, and the list goes on. You obviously can't shut out all media from her, so you should guide her by explaining the differences between the 'real world' and that professional world of glamour.

Fitting in is an important part of being thirteen. So there is one aspect that influences body image from up close and challenges all parents – the peer group. When she goes to school every day, she looks at the popular girls and the older girls and compares her body with theirs. Even if your daughter has her own group of friends and is reasonably well-liked among her schoolmates, the chances are that she will not like something about the way she looks. Parents have the job of stepping in when her preoccupation with changing her looks goes beyond the occasional whining.

Peers are a teenager's life. In fact, research done at Texas A&M University (USA) illustrated this. Researchers had recruited 237 girls from the ages of ten to seventeen. They were asked to name their three favorite TV shows and to rate the attractiveness of the female actresses in those shows. This was to measure their exposure to the Hollywood ideal of beauty. Then the researchers evaluated the girls' body weight and height, their use of social media and their feelings of inferiority in response to other girls. In addition to this, the girls were asked how they felt about their bodies, whether they had any symptoms of an eating disorder and how satisfied they were with their lives overall. The process was repeated six months later.

Here's what they found: The girls' TV exposure and social media use did not predict eating disorder symptoms. Surprisingly, these factors did not predict body dissatisfaction either. Peer competition was the factor that appeared to significantly influence body dissatisfaction and, in the long term, predict eating disorder symptoms. This lead them to conclude in the *Journal of Youth and Adolescence* that "[t]his suggests that peer competition is more salient to body and eating issues in teenage girls."

Although India has had a limited number of studies on

teenage body image, there has been one with results that re-emphasise how harmful negative body image can be. This research study conducted on almost 600 girls from age ten to nineteen in Lucknow, Uttar Pradesh, concluded that the girls who already thought that they were too thin, still wanted to be thinner. Think about that for a minute. A girl who is thin and trying to lose weight can end up falling very ill from over exercise or extreme dieting or whichever method she chooses to reach her unreasonable goal.

So you find yourself witnessing an 'everybody wants to be Barbie' phenomenon. This controversial doll has been hated by parents for promoting unhealthy body image in girls. A recent National Public Radio[1] article mentions that psychologists have said that playing with a Barbie doll for even just a few minutes can cause the girl to limit her career ambitions. That sounds scary but an artist called Nickolay Lamm is trying to change things. He plans to create a doll with minimal makeup, shorts and a simple blouse. His version of the doll will represent the dimensions of actual young women in the United States. Lamm has good reason to be behind the creation of this doll. He has a female cousin who had negative body image which prevented her from having the courage to put on a swimsuit. So parents can expect 'Barbie' to have a healthier body type and be ethnically diverse someday soon.

For now, just be alert for worrying behaviour such as criticism of her looks and body, frequent comparison of her body with other girls and women, and obsessive thoughts about losing weight. There could even be a phasc where she won't want to leave the house because she thinks she is too fat. Don't ignore the signs.

1 National Public Radio is a famous radio station located in the United States of America

Rashmi Uday Singh's Story

13

First things first; I hate preaching. This is simply because I am still learning and have a long way to go. What I will do now is share some of my experiences and hope that they hold some relevance in your life. When I turned thirteen, I expected to feel like a 'teenager', whatever that meant. The word sounded attractive to someone like me who had a conservative upbringing and wasn't even allowed to talk to boys, but somehow I felt grown up. I wasn't even allowed near any members of the opposite sex.

My school and college were both all girls' institutions. The first boy I met was at age nineteen and he became my husband. But through it all, what I loved most was my convent boarding school where the power of prayer was deeply ingrained in me. One of the important lessons that I learnt back then, was to pray in gratitude and to pray when in trouble. The lesson holds true even today. I also learnt that only sheep roam in herds and look for security in each other. On the other hand, tigers are happy on their own. Basically, I never belonged to any clique in school and interacted with everybody as I do now.

I see a huge difference between my generation and the current one. Thirteen-year-olds in my time, didn't face the challenges of dressing up, having fancy birthday parties or getting mobile phones from their parents. Body image is another common challenge but didn't affect me thankfully. I'm trying to be friends with my wrinkles though. Being brought up in a Punjabi family, it was commonplace for my uncles to mince no words about appearances, cracking jokes about my fat nose and other shortcomings. So, while I was highly conscious of my ordinary looks, it never really bothered me on a deep level.

Physical appearance doesn't mean anything at all. True beauty is from within. The beauty that is associated with a person's enthusiasm and kindness. My mom always told me '*shakal acchi nahi te gal acchi kiya kar*', which translates as 'If you don't look beautiful, at least speak kind words.' I've always been comfortable with my body but am yet to make friends with my wrinkles.

I enjoyed competitive sports including basketball and badminton. I also swam for my school and state teams. Sports can be fun while giving you good exercise. I would advise you to participate in them. When you are physically fit, your mind feels good too. Playing sports does wonders for your confidence and overall health. Fitness is vital for teenagers.

Parents need to be empathic to their daughters. You have to realise that your daughter is extremely conscious of her physical traits. The best way to drive home your message about being healthy is to peg it on that. I am not for a moment suggesting that you should make her believe that appearances are everything, but handle the matter with sensitivity and put yourself in her shoes. For example, you shouldn't call them Tips for Healthy Eating. In its place, say they are Tips for Looking Good. This will make a difference in the way she perceives your advice. She will probably feel like you want to help her be popular and happy. There's no problem if her health improves in the process, right?

When you try to introduce healthy eating patterns in your teen's life, remember that you are role models for her. Set an example by eating right and light too. Practise what you preach. If she sees you eating oily *paranthas* and *laddus* every night, she won't take your advice seriously.

You could also think of new ways to create healthy meals. This could involve adapting old family recipes to newer cooking methods. The usual oily fish in gravy could be substituted with fish grilled in the convection oven. Light stir fry preparations could replace the normal masala You could also think of new ways to create healthy meals. This could involve adapting old family recipes to newer cooking methods. The usual oily fish in gravy could be substituted with fish grilled in the convection oven. Light stir fry preparations could replace the normal masala laden *subzi*. Baking and boiling food instead of deep frying it, can promise good health. When you explain the changes to your daughter, say 'good figure'. That is a primary concern in the thirteen-year-old girl's mind.

There are other good habits that can make her look better and therefore, feel better about herself and life in general. So here's my advice for the girls who have just begun their teens:

Do you want your face to glow? It's simple. All you have to do is to make it a point to drink many glasses of water a day. It will purify your body's whole system by kicking out unwanted toxins. Drinking a lot of water also helps by causing more urination, which has the side benefit of getting rid of weight. Fruit is needed too. I never ate fruits regularly when I was growing up. Sadly, my boarding school barely served a banana a day. I still regret not eating enough fruits. Not surprisingly, my mother-in-law and grandmother-in-law have glowing, clear complexions and great health too, because they live on fruit. The same fruit-filled diet gave my Ammaji a healthy face that was glowing till the day that she passed away in her late nineties.

How do you become the most energetic girl on the playground? Eat a large, healthy and balanced breakfast. It gives you just the right fuel to kick start your day. I suggest fruit, eggs, milk, oatmeal, whole wheat toast and lightly sautéed sprouts. You can take your pick.

Are you worried about your body being too fat? Do remember that your body image is how you think and feel about your body. It is not always the reality because body image involves your thoughts, perception, imagination and emotions. It's a vicious cycle. When you have a poor body image, you diet, you exercise too much to the point that you become ill and you end up having eating disorders. In the long run, these events lead to not just a poor body image, but a lousy looking body. Yo-yo dieting can make you physically and mentally sick. You don't want to be depressed. You also don't want to be what you dread the most-being fat. Also, remember that weight loss from dieting does not last. You need to exercise. It works hand in hand.

I'm sure you agree with me when I say that snack attacks are a real nuisance. So how can you stop the snack attacks? The obvious answer is to skip junk food but equally important is to snack on foods that add to your nutrition instead of adding empty calories that don't even satisfy your hunger. So what do you eat when you are hungry between meals? Reach for a piece of fruit, a handful of nuts or breakfast granola. These will keep your hunger pangs away and prevent you from bingeing on food such as wafers, pizzas and burgers.

Now I'm going to sound like a real preachy grandma but have learnt this through years of experience. What you eat is important but so is the time and place where you are eating.

Please Do NOT sit down to eat while you're talking on the phone or busy on the computer or in front of the television set. There's a valid reason for this warning. If you eat while you're focused on another activity, you will eat too much without even realising it. More food means extra calories that will punish you in the form of added inches on your body.

How often you eat determines your body weight and health too. Skipping meals doesn't help your body. Eating at regular intervals does. Do not eat heavy meals that make you feel bloated and sluggish. Instead, eat smaller meals to keep yourself satisfied and full of energy for school and fun.

The speed at which you eat your food plays a part in keeping your body healthy and good looking. Eat slowly. This fact cannot be emphasised enough. Not only will eating slowly help you digest your food better, but it will also make you feel full faster. The brain gets signals of satiety from receptors in the stomach wall and when you eat slowly, these signals reach the brain and prevent you from over-eating. If you eat too fast, you will fill yourself with more food because you aren't giving your brain enough time to get the signals. Makes sense, I hope?

Last but not the least; you have to junk the junk food. It is called Junk Food for a good reason. If you want to look good, then leave out fizzy drinks like colas from your diet. Potato chips, pizza, French fries and anything else that you call fast food must be avoided. They are high in all the bad things - sugar, salt and fat. They also contain low amounts of the good things including fibre and nutrients such as calcium and iron which are essential for a healthy body.

I hope this helps keep you in shape and content with your healthy body. Remember that a body that looks best is a body which is healthy. Above all enjoy and thank God for all the goodies. You shall never be young and thirteen again. Enjoy.

Ishi Khosla's Story

13

When I was a teenager, I wanted to be a good student. I wanted to be smart, slim, good looking and confident. Unfortunately, I was fat. It was probably my strong desire to be slim and better looking that enabled me to lose all my excess weight. It was ironic that when I was trying to lose the kilos, my healthy lifestyle changes seemed completely unnecessary to many.

Traditional Punjabis are fond of wholesome, ample figures that are often a symbol of wealth and good health. I remember one distant relative commenting in Punjabi, "*Kudi maadi hogayi hai*!" To them, this meant that my newly slim body was a negative change. I was taken aback that anybody could say such a thing because I thought I looked much better than before. Plus, I felt a lot more confident about myself. It is still common for older generations in India to equate fat with being healthy, but this did not discourage or deter me.

I don't remember any external factors bothering me about my figure, but I certainly did not like the way that I looked – especially in my school uniform skirts. I guess I am aesthetically sensitive and appreciate beauty in all forms, including a fit body. I was determined and managed to lose all my weight by the time I was fifteen. Most people find it hard to believe that the reason I chose my career is rooted in my own weight problem during my childhood. When I look back at those years as an obese child, I can still see my cousins calling me 'fatty'.

It wasn't as if I was taking good care of my health. I often ate breakfast twice and was always ready for good food. I would wait with my mouth half open for blobs of fresh white butter, which my mother churned out regularly. The truth is, our home was all about gourmet food, from bakery to traditional delicacies and basics, and everything was made at home. Home-made ice-cream, breads, pizzas, cakes, cookies, desserts, jams, jellies, pickles, rasgulla, ras-malai, samosas, chaat and potato wafers - we had it all.

My father was a chemistry specialist and my mother a home scientist, so perhaps, concerns about hygiene and safety kept our kitchen busy and our dining table full of fresh goodies. This also fostered a scientific temper around food and terms like trans-fatty acids, melting points, freezing points and coal-tar dyes were used often. Following that environment at home, it was not surprising that I became hugely interested in food and took to baking when I was just eight years old.

A few years later, when I was around twelve, I started writing and documenting my recipes. By then, I had become aware of my excess weight and had started counting calories. My cousins gave me company. Together, we became completely obsessed with calculating how much we ate and how many calories we had managed to burn. If we ate more, we jogged extra.

If we ate too many calories one day, we decided to compensate the next day by consuming fewer calories. Dinners had almost reduced to just a fruit or soup. Soon enough, with that discipline, I lost all my excess weight and remember being called 'thinny-pinny' by my English teacher. That was when I dropped the idea of studying medicine despite having chosen the medical stream already. Hooked onto the subject of nutrition science, I altered my life's path and joined Lady Irwin College. It is from there that I graduated with a Masters in Foods and Nutrition.

So being fat changed my life. Or you could say that losing my fat changed my life and motivated me to research the underlying science of food and nutrition. Having extra fat on your body is certainly not an 'in' thing. It carries with it much baggage and a social stigma. The stereotype of a female is certainly slim and not fat, so overweight girls are likely to feel negativity and inadequate.

Many young girls go through psychological issues centered on their body type. Eating disorders are quick to develop and these, including anorexia and bulimia, are actually psychological problems manifesting in altered eating behaviour. . If not dealt with at an early stage, they can be life threatening because the body image is only one part of the cause. I have seen patients, both boys and girls, suffering from these disorders and multiple unresolved issues can exist to create such harmful behaviour.

My message to parents and educators is to develop your child's self-esteem, creating a self worth, with a focus on fitness, mental and physical well-being and healthy eating habits from early childhood. Girls, you should engage in healthy co-existence with your peers rather than unhealthy competition. Always remember that you are unique! Make sure you include good food in your daily diet.

This list includes whole grains, pulses, low fat dairy, plenty of vegetables and fruits, lean meats, fish and nuts. Dairy is a vital component of a young girl's diet. Ensure that you have about 2-3 servings of dairy products (milk / yogurt / paneer/ cheese) in your diet to meet nutritional requirements at this age. Seek professional advice, in case you are sensitive to dairy.

Have indulgence food sparingly. When I say indulgence food, I refer to food meant for special occasions like cupcakes, bakery products, puddings, pies and desserts. Minimise intake of processed foods like crisps, processed breakfast cereals and snack food. Healthy snacking should include fresh fruits, salads, sprouts, yogurt, nuts and seeds.

Don't forget that looking good isn't just about a healthy body weight. Glowing, healthy skin is an aspect of looking good too. Acne is a common feature at this age. Make sure to include Vitamin A rich foods in your diet. These include spinach, tomatoes, carrots, pumpkin, papaya and dried apricots to name a few. For a blemish free skin, cut back on sugar, bad fat (trans-fats) and junk food. Include plenty of fluids and water.

Beware of the effects of changing hormonal balances as well. With the hormone activity at this age, your chances of putting on weight are high. You need to be active and be physically active- jog, swim or engage in any sport of your choice. Parents must be extra cautious about supervising her meals during her periods because increased requirements of certain nutrients especially iron.

With all that said, I hope you don't plan to go to any extremes to lose your extra weight because aiming to lose too much weight in a short duration is unreasonable and can make it counterproductive. A realistic weight loss goal is 2 to 3 kilograms per month. Eating right and regular exercise helps you lose weight, look and feel good.

Chapter 10

Choosing Your Role Models

A thirteen-year-old girl needs a role model or two. This person is the one who she will try to be like. Sometimes the role model becomes an idol when respect and liking turn into blind admiration and devotion that can border on obsession. While a lot of girls choose to emulate a parent or teacher at first, the role model changes as they get older because their priorities change. From looking up to parents since birth, the focus has shifted to pleasing the peers. So girls who admire a friendly teacher or a character from a Disney movie, will move her attention to those who are physically attractive, with nice hair and makeup, but with a fair degree of talent as well. Her role model could be sitting in the same school building, in another classroom.

Juniors can find a lot of things to admire in seniors who have moved past the awkward stage and blossomed into the slim, pretty popular ones with what seems like perfect hair and a perfect social life. Research has shown that popularity and looks go well together. This means that role models have to look good – or have the physical characteristics determined by social norms.

There's a change in the kind of personalities teen role models have as the girls get older. It could be that she used to idolise the middle-aged, makeup-free, overweight TV anchor of a science show in her tweens, but now she does her best to look and talk like Alia Bhatt ever since she saw her latest movie. And why not, she would say. The actress is one of the youngest in the film industry, so there's the connection of young age. Then there are the signs of success shouting out from magazines and the screen. If somebody looks great and is popular, your teen thinks she has found her method to success.

Dr. Amy Beth Taublieb, a clinical psychologist in the United States shared her experiences on Disney's family.com website. Taublieb has observed that teenagers choose their role models based on what they lack themselves. So, if you think that your hair is too curly and ugly, you, the teenager, will find yourself a role model who has smooth, long tresses. This is actually a message to the parents. You can easily find out which part of her she is unhappy with.

The trouble stems from parents and the daughter disagreeing on good role models versus the bad, unhealthy ones. It all depends on what your daughter and her peers think is cool. For instance, she and her closest friends may believe that using foul language is a way to impress everybody at school. So then they will start treating the older children who use bad language, like they are objects of worship. As they continue to worship these role models, they will imitate them and become copycats. It won't just be about the distasteful vocabulary then because they will want to look like them and walk like them and talk like them – to be exactly like them.

When a parent sees things heading in this direction, conflict cannot be avoided. If you smell trouble you need to explain to your teen that her role model or idol has disrespectful behaviour and that she is supporting indecent behaviour by giving him or her so much attention. Even though she thinks that she has to be liked at any cost, you have to sit her down and tell her precisely why her current role models are not right for her. Don't push other potential role models at her. She will take time to understand why she has been told to stop emulating somebody she thinks is perfect.

Young teens need their peers to tell them that they are appreciated. Parents, you will miss those days when she came to ask you for every opinion. "Mom, how do you like my dress?" Or, "Daddy, which book should I read? Don't feel unloved. You have already accomplished the big job of constructing her foundation. The values that you have instilled in her since day one on earth, won't disappear if you keep communication open and let her grow.

In fact, you both need to retain your role of role models by setting an example of healthy behaviour and lifestyle. Whether it is eating healthy meals or giving blankets and food to homeless people and animals in her neighbourhood, everything you say and do, informs her of what is appropriate behaviour in the family.

Don't lose your firmness with her, but remember that she still needs your guidance and wants you to be her friend, more than a critical, dominating dictator. You can help her choose positive role models by giving her books with strong female characters. A female detective, who is popular because she solves mysteries with her problem solving skills, travels all over the world, and gets recognition from authorities including the police and international governments, would seem pretty cool once your daughter is hooked onto the books. Share magazine articles with her if you see positive role models featured in them. Interviews of female business owners, artists and scientists can bring on an interest in a previously unknown possibility. "Mom, can I sell the greetings cards that I make? She may ask.

Tell her about the celebrities who don't just pose with expensive coffee and their current boyfriends. Celebrities raising funds for a cause can make better role models than the ones who are always in the news for scandals. Recently, Kalki Koechlin was in the news for a short film dedicated to women's rights. Nandita Das was part of a major campaign that dared to say Dark is Beautiful. There are plenty of women to choose from. You can give her the exposure and then let her choose.

Try introducing her to older children you know, who are studying in college or university, or who have just started working. Once they she sits across from them and sees their confident manner of speaking, she will want to hear more about what they do and how fun college can be. Who knows, during this time when her brain is working overtime to figure out things, a conversation can spark off motivation that lasts for a long time.

Tanusree Shankar's Story

13

For me and every other thirteen-year-old girl, finally embarking on our teens was a relief! In fact, it was the beginning of a new, special chapter in our lives. At thirteen, we began our journey of curiosity and inquisitiveness. I remember bodily changes being a major part of the experience. Wider, deepening hips and the formation of breasts were all a part of coming closer to womanhood. My first bra was a cause for excitement.

As we graduated from slips and undershirts to the much awaited undergarment, my female classmates and I formed a special bond. Of course there were cliques at school and competition for boys, but everything was forgotten when that topic came up. Maybe it was because we felt special being able to wear what all the older girls had been wearing for ages. Or perhaps it was our hidden fear.

By fear, I mean the doubts and insecurity that came with the new 'us'. Sometimes the thirteen -year-old girl can get overwhelmed with the changes. For example, some of my friends worried that they were too fat or their breasts were too small. At thirteen, the body becomes a major focus.

Even with the concern for body image – which exists for thirteen-year-olds even today – our expectations were not as high as compared to teenage girls now. Back then, there was the usual pressure from parents and teachers to study hard and get good grades, but we never thought of life as a challenge. 'Challenge' is a big word. It is a word that hints at a difficult phase of life. Fortunately for me and other girls in my time, we could always turn to our parents, teachers and grandparents for guidance.

The joint-family model isn't that popular these days and young girls often consider only their peers as their guides. In other words, thirteen-year-olds today are more mature and much ahead of where we were in those days. I think that the main reason for this difference lies in the exposure that today's teenagers have. When I was thirteen, television did not exist. The only entertainment we had was the radio. To add to this, was the limited number of channels and selected listening decided by our parents.

Observing so much, reading so many things, having access to opinion makers on digital media, thirteen-year-olds have the opportunity to pick up much more than we did at this young age. Tips on dressing up, role models to affect their style of speaking, and popular opinions on every possible topic – today's thirteen-year-old has no dearth of information to process.

The girls I see have a different body language. One might say that they seem less like children than the old days. Their value system seems to be quite different as well. They seem to be planning ahead in a big way because they know their minds before they step into thirteen. In our case, we were always advised by our parents regarding our future plans and would listen to them without any questions asked. So, the current thirteen-year-old has a prominent independent streak. She's ambitious too. This may be why children seem more stressed these days. The quest for success in every aspect of life – appearance, social standing, and career – begins much earlier than in our time.

Honestly, during my thirteenth year, I did not think of life so seriously that I would understand the lessons coming my way. But years down the line, I am grateful. My parents were my support. They gave me a sheltered life with constant guidance and advice whenever it was needed. We lead a simple, uncomplicated life, so the question of solving challenges never came up for me.

I especially value the guidance that my mother gave me during that crucial phase of my life. Whatever became ingrained in me has helped me to pass on good values to my daughter, Sreenanda. My mother was my idol. Her name was Rina Ghosh Choudhury. She was a woman with the strongest personality. While most girls wouldn't like a strict mother, I believe that her strict, disciplinarian nature is a reason why I am who I am today. Plus, I grew up in an Army household where a disciplined life was natural.

I learnt to respect elders and be polite with Everyone – elders, youngsters, not-so-old people, and that included servants. Through the lessons that I learnt, I came to the conclusion that if you are kind to people, you will feel happy and healthy yourself. But of course, the kindness has to come from within. It has to be felt and not just be some automatic gestures or words. My father always reminded me of that.

To make sure that I was well-rounded, my mother made a habit of giving me tasks to complete. For example, on Saturday I had to do all the dusting in the house, make the beds, and lay the table for meals, along with other household chores. Although I didn't enjoy the forced activity at first, I later figured out that this was my mother training me in her own way. Somehow, I started enjoying the routine. Not only did she inculcate in me the habit of keeping neat and tidy rooms, but her tasks pushed me towards more creative pursuits like rearranging the furniture in various ways or using flowers as decoration. My mother said: God resides in cleanliness.

Along with my mother, my father was a wonderful teacher too. I thought he was a saint. I always looked up to him and continue to be inspired by the example that he set for me. His patience was a trait that I admired and attempted to inherit. I think I have learnt it well. Another important lesson that my father taught me is deep-rooted in me: never criticise anybody. His explanation was: when you point a finger towards a person, three fingers point back at you. What he meant was that the best thing to do was to work sincerely and not waste time or energy caring about what others around you were doing. "Do your best and leave the rest," he would say. The idea of staying quiet instead of pointing out the flaws in others seemed hard when I was that young. But once I was older, I realised the significance of these values passed onto me.

Another person who molded me into what I am today was Ananda Shankar. My 13 was a beautiful and memorable one because that's when I met him. I got married to him at a young age. In other words, I grew up with him. He was my idol and mentor in the field of art and culture and in my career too. Indeed, Ananda was the pillar in my life. Being thirteen years older, he guided and protected me at every step from the moment that we met.

Interestingly, when I had joined the Uday Shankar India Culture Center in 1969, Ananda was in the United States and I had not even known that Mamata (Shankar) had a brother or that Mashima (Amala Shankar) had a son! I first saw him on 10th January, 1970, when he returned from Los Angeles and found myself immediately interested in this very good looking man who had just cut an album with Warner Music in LA. Ananda had just introduced the world to what he called World Music. As a thirteen-year-old, I was awestruck and quite conscious of his presence. But that was it. My focus back then was dance and only dance.

But of course, then I fell in love. After that, I faced the challenge of having to convince my parents and elders that what I felt was love and not mere infatuation. This idol of mine was clearly aware of the family he was born into but focused on making his parents feel proud of his personal achievements. I loved the way he wanted to make it on his own merit and not as Uday Shankar's son or as Pandit Ravi Shankar's nephew. That sincerity and determination had me smitten.

Gradually, the same level of resolve urged me to let out any talent that had been hiding inside of me. Ananda's talent in the field of music was another reason that I found myself in love with him. He would say, "This is going to be the music of tomorrow." He was right. Spending time with my idol helped me pick up his many qualities which included patriotism, self-confidence, a belief in hard work and perseverance, and commitment to people. Along with those, I managed to adopt his respect for punctuality, a sense of humour, compassion for others, and an ability to make impartial judgments. All of these things contributed to my successful career and personal life. I continue to follow Ananda's example every day.

Some years later, I remember the time when Ananda came to our house with his proposal of marriage. My parents were not impressed by his famous surname. Instead, they wanted to ask him about his plans for earning a livelihood. Ananda was touched. Here were a girl's parents who were not giving their daughter away easily even though they knew about his well-known family. That day my respect for my parents went up even higher. In fact, my admiration for my other idol, Ananda, increased as well because he obviously cared a lot about everybody's happiness.

There was the time when I was still very young and I got my first assignment as a choreographer for the opening ceremony of the International Pacific Asia Travel Association conference in Delhi. I was extremely nervous. Ananda kept on encouraging me as always by saying that I needed to take this first step in order to understand my potential. I was surprised at the confidence that he had in me. He told me, "The audience will come to see your work the first time because you are Uday Shankar and Amala Shankar's daughter-in-law and Ananda Shankar's wife, but if they don't like your work, they will NOT return."

Well, I guess I was lucky because I have kept on working since 1978 till date. And even though he isn't with me physically, I get strong support from Ananda spiritually. At times, I wonder if he was mentoring and preparing me as he knew that he would be leaving earlier. Whatever little I have been able to achieve in my professional life happened because of the path that Ananda showed me.

While I had my idols right by my side, I remember friends who chose more distant idols like Bollywood or Hollywood celebrities or foreign writers. There were some classmates who kept a picture of their idol in their rooms. Others would silently keep track of their idols and do their best to emulate their ways. Whether your role model or idol is with you or far away, having an idol with positive qualities can teach you a lot and push you towards progress. All the things that you admire and love about your idol transfer to you through watching, believing and learning. But I believe that actively looking out for an idol isn't important.

What is important is for thirteen-year-olds to look up to their parents and to listen to them. Parents are your well-wishers and the best source of honest guidance. Basically, they really do have nothing but your interests in mind. Thirteen is a vulnerable age. It is an age where children are able to learn, absorb and appreciate values that stay on for life. I believe that thirteen-year-olds should trust their parents and allow them to lead the way. Don't forget that your parents have gone through the same experiences so they know about all the hurdles and how to overcome them. If you do this, I know you will be happy, safe and successful!

Chapter 11

Making Downtime Positive

Your teen's leisure hours are a luxury. Those evenings between homework and sleep and the weekends give her ample time for relaxation. When you think about relaxing teenagers, you probably visualise her taking a nap or with her eyes peeled on the computer, chatting with friends, but her downtime can be quite productive if you decide to introduce some structured activity into her schedule. That doesn't mean that naps and socialising should be stopped completely. It just means that she can do both.

Your child is under a lot of pressure when she is thirteen. It isn't just her peers who expect her to be a certain way. Parental expectations can lead to immense stress too. For example, imagine the pressure on a girl whose parents insist that she doesn't take even a day's break from practicing her classical dance. The girl could have days where she wants to lie around doing nothing, or she could be plain tired.

If you are not sensitive to her needs, she can be more stressed out than normal. The same applies to the girl who is reprimanded and criticised whenever her A pluses become A minuses. That is a huge burden to take for a thirteen-year-old. And the expectations are more than earlier generations with more choices in an education and career bringing in extra competition from an early age. So a teenager needs to have something fun and useful to do other than having her nose buried in her textbooks.

Studies have shown that children involved in activities outside the academic curriculum perform better at school. Researchers have attributed this result to the experience that the girls get in learning time management, being stress-free and their motivation to do well in more than one thing. Another observation has been that the children who play sports learn to work in groups because teamwork involves learning about cooperation and communication.

According to researchers, students who participate in extracurricular activities are likely to see better academic performance and life skills such as discipline, goal-setting and teamwork.

Additionally, they learn to be accountable for their behaviour and actions, while taking on responsibility. All this is not surprising when you think of your teen finding herself in a situation outside home and school, interacting with strangers and knowing that she has to prove herself in a new setting. And with colleges abroad and in India looking closely at applicants' non academic history along with their grades, this is a great time to start building that profile. It's never too early to think about higher education.

Your daughter's leisure time does not have to be completely structured; it should be fun too. If one extracurricular activity doesn't turn out to be as interesting and fun for her, try another one because if she is not keen on doing something, her desire to do well will disappear. Once she stops taking an interest in it, she won't try hard enough to excel at it and nor will she learn any skills from it. Limit her activities to one or two to prevent over scheduling and making her feel exhausted. The idea is to keep her happy and productive.

Family time is a part of hanging loose. Try to keep at least one meal a day for your family for the end of day bonding where you can talk about her life. If she wants to talk about school, let her. But discussing the effects of pollution or a documentary you saw on TV can foster thinking outside the box. Plus, spending free time regularly with her keeps you all connected during an age where she can easily distance herself and never talk to anybody but her friends.

If you decide to go watch a movie, you can ask her for a verbal movie review later. That would actually help develop her skills of analysis.If you take her to a concert or an art show, she may want to follow up the visit with online research on the artists whose work she saw. That's knowledge again. You could also try an alternative to eating out and cook together. She may end up enjoying herself and can learn to help out in the house like this. And think of the unhealthy fast food so many teens eat these days; this activity could encourage health eating in the long run.

Emphasize the importance of being a well-rounded person. Tell her that school is very important and so are relationships with people, fun with friends and physical activity. She can cycle around the neighbourhood. She can join tennis or soccer classes. She can volunteer for a cause. It maybe that an old neighbour would like your child to read out loud to her, or just visit her to chat. Compassion can teach a teenager to look at life beyond just 'me'.

Get your daughter to switch off her gadgets and computer for a while. Being online every waking minute is not healthy. You could keep a day fixed for family time when everything has to be turned off. Never forget that she needs intellectual stimulation to go with her good grades and extracurricular activities.

Downtime is a good time to take a seat next to her and talk. You can share something that you've read in a magazine with her. Or you may ask her to tell you about something that she has learned from her non academic activities. You may find yourself having a discussion about basketball, followed by a conversation about well-known basketball players and then a question-answer session once she is more interested. If she likes to play board games, start a ritual of chess or any other game that promotes skills of strategy.

There are girls who don't like being busy with anything other than their school work and friends. Initially, these teens need to be coerced into doing anything in their leisure time. There's one sentence you can use to make her see reason: If you apply to college with nothing else but good grades to show, they won't admit you. Essentially, she has to be aware of the fact that she has to spread herself and her interests a bit for her own well being and future.

Preeti Vyas's Story

13

When I look at myself today as a contented adult, happy in my own skin, finally satisfied professionally and personally, I realise that certain elements of my childhood contribute to who I am now. It is true that all the things that define my life today, including my career path, what I do to beat stress, and things that I live for, took their roots when I was a young girl.

It's almost like I had to spend my 20s and 30s exploring whatever lay untouched, to come back to the realisation that I am still the same at 40 as I was at thirteen! In his book called *Outliers*, author Malcolm Gladwell wrote that it's easy to make the connection between your aptitude as a child and who you are as an adult. Sometimes you'll see a successful doctor become an accomplished painter, or a high profile banker turn into a bestselling author. When you look back at their childhood, the signs are obvious.

When I was growing up, I found out how much travel rejuvenated me. My most vivid memory of being thirteen was of my first trip abroad with my family. We went to Europe. The experience was magical. Seeing new cultures, old cathedrals and universities, the Eiffel Tower in Paris – these wonderful places changed my view of the world. I had always been a travel buff and went on every school trip from the age of eight, but this was a whole new level of exposure and novelty.

The shorter school trips lasted just two or three days but I loved getting away from the routine of school life, especially the pressure of academics. I cherished the freedom and felt proud of the faith, trust and confidence that my parents had in me. Remember, these were the days before mobile phones came into our lives. One postcard was the norm back then. While seeing new places taught me to look at the world from different perspectives, it also taught me to be happy in my own company. I was quite satisfied singing songs and playing antakshari with my gang of friends at these trips, but also felt quite content staring out of a train or bus window for hours.

During one such trip to Nepal, our bus met with an accident on a treacherous Himalayan cliff. Fortunately, the bus fell flat on the cliff-side and not on the valley-side. It was an important growing-up moment for me. There we were, a bunch of thirteen-year-old girls stuck on a mountain road in the middle of the night, having only just escaped death. Instead of scaring me away from travel, the incident made me want to travel more for the thrills and adventure attached to it.

As a student in Australia, I travelled extensively and loved the freedom of travelling alone in a new country. My travels brought me close to photography, writing, and music. These are activities that I still value in my busy adult life. Trips can be refreshing and educational experiences. They don't need to be elaborate or expensive. Spontaneous outings within your city can be fun. As a teenager (and even today), I would often just jump onto a local train and get off at a station that I had never been to before. After a while, I felt thrilled knowing that my feet had walked on a part of my city that I had never seen before - despite spending most of my life there. I remember walking around the surrounding market area, enjoying the view of a marketplace full of delicious vegetable and fruits, buying a small trinket as a souvenir. I would love to guess which the dominant community in that area was on the basis of the fresh produce being sold in the markets near the station. I would then usually have a quick dosa or a vada pav and get back on the train.

And that's how you could get yourself a short but enriching vacation by yourself! My advice to all girls would be to take time off to do unplanned things which stretch your mind and expose you to a new way of life. It will energise you in a way you cannot imagine. My dream has always been to see as many countries of the world as possible. Every year, I aim for a new one. It is helpful that I have a husband and child who share my passion for travel. We would be happy to go without new clothes for a year in exchange for the opportunity to visit a new country.

Other than travelling, another interest that was fun and productive too, was entrepreneurship. Yes, my entrepreneurial spirit started when I was a child and is of course a large part of my adult life. When I was about twelve in the 80s, my dad bought me a computer. It was brand new in the market and called the Sinclair ZX Spectrum. The computer had only four or five programmes. Even the simplest smart phone today can do more than what that huge machine could do.

Along with the ubiquitous 'Pacman', one of the programmes on the computer created horoscopes. All you had to do is punch in your name and birth date and the machine would eject several pages that would contain details of your personality and your future. With my Dad's encouragement, I began printing out customised horoscopes for my school friends for the substantial sum of Rs. 20 each. I continued selling them until the novelty wore off as we all began to eventually realise that the horoscopes were essentially a random selection of the same 100 odd personality and future descriptions. My various entrepreneurial ventures were more like 'uptime' because they left me so energised.

I even tried to earn money doing odd jobs. For instance, my father would pay me Rs. 2 for each dividend deposit slip that I filled out for him. Later on, in my college days, my best friend and I set up stalls at the fests to sell brownies and pastries that we baked the previous night. In my late teens, I often took up small catering assignments where I'd cook pasta and risotto for my sister's friends' parties. All that said, it is important to develop a good relationship with money; to learn how to earn it and create wealth. No matter what you choose to do in life, whether you choose to be in a creative field like writing or painting, or join the corporate world, you will need to interact with money. There's no escaping it.

Earning money always excited me because I was determined to be financially independent. As a young student in Australia, I was doing *all* of the following in addition to my full time course; being International Students' Advisor at my hostel, tutoring first year students, waitressing at a restaurant at weekends and working at a large department store, ToysRUs. It was exhilarating to be able to do it all and earn my own upkeep! When I was 26, I started my own independent bookshop called Kidztown. Today, I am still an entrepreneur. I believe that being financially independent is very important. Somehow, girls in India are conditioned to not take this seriously. They are often made to believe that there will always be a man to provide for them. I think that educated girls who have spent so many years in academic life must do something with that education and be equal partners in the financial responsibilities of running a home when they grow up. Finding the right boyfriend or husband is not the only critical aspect of your life. In fact one can survive happily without one, as many of my single friends will vouch. But finding a way to earn money is vital.

Along with travel and my early entrepreneurial activities, books took up a lot of my relaxation time. "Mamma, you have a bookshop in your tummy", said my four-year-old son recently. He isn't far off from the truth. I am surrounded by books, both at work and at home. I grew up in a house full of books amidst a family of passionate readers. So, it is not surprising that I was reading from a young age and reading all genres. Before I reached nine, I had devoured all the Enid Blytons, with the Enchanted Wood and The Secret Seven being my favourites. By the time I was thirteen, I was reading everything that I could lay my hands on.

Since my Dad was a doctor, he read a lot of scientific journals among various other subjects. My mom read books on spirituality. I consumed it all, from Scientific American, National Geographic and MAD, to Autobiography of a Yogi and Living with the Himalayan Masters to a whole spectrum of comics. I can safely say that books have been the surest, most entertaining and most dependable friends I have had through my life. I can also tell you with confidence that there is not a single problem in the world that you would encounter in your daily life, whose solutions you won't find within the pages of a book.

Books have helped me deal with many hairpin bends in life, right from dealing with life in a new country, to caring for my newborn son, to dealing with my Dad's sudden death. Books are not only a good way to spend leisure hours, but they can be an advisor and companion during tough times. As a teenager it was easy to get carried away by the crowd, to want to conform to standards of dressing, hairstyles and even behaviour displayed by the so called 'cool' crowd. The effect continued later on in college, when I was the only one among my group of friends who didn't take the CAT exam for admission to the IIMs During those years, my love for books helped me remain my own person and decide the best path for me, even if I was the only one choosing that road.

.After reading all these memories would you be surprised to know that I'm a forty-year-old woman who lives to travel for new experiences, reads a lot and makes a living running her own business selling children's books?

All I can say is that the answers to the questions of who you will become, what path you will choose, and what things and experiences will make you happy are already around you. All you need to do is look inside. Don't spend all your time worrying about that A or A plus. Use your free time to read, to go out and explore and experience new things. Remember that in most cases, like me, you will find lasting happiness at the point where you first began.

SPECIAL FEATURE

Fun in the Kitchen with POOJA DHINGRA

The first proper kitchen memory that I have is from when I was just seven years old. I was spending the weekend at my aunt's house. Since I was an impatient child, she had to keep thinking of new ways to keep me entertained. One day she called me to her kitchen and said that I was old enough to learn how to bake brownies.

I remember laying out the ingredients on her kitchen counter. My small hands reached out for flour, butter, sugar and eggs. These were magic ingredients. The steps were right there in front of us and all we had to do was follow them. Dollops of butter whisked with beautiful crystallised specs of brown sugar. Light and fluffy eggs whisked till they doubled in volume and then gently mixed with chocolate - the memory of the aroma still makes me sigh. The batter looked gorgeous and almost like it had a mind of its own while it spread itself in the 8-inch baking tray. We tossed walnuts on top and put it in the oven.

I still remember checking the oven every five minutes to see if they were ready. "Patience," my aunt told me. "A good baker needs to be patient. Do your magic, put it in the oven and then leave it." A comforting buttery aroma filled the room. In 30 minutes we removed the cake tin from the oven.

I stared at the beautiful crisp top. The nuts we tossed on top were the perfect shade of brown. We cut a slice of the gooey cake and I was mesmerised. I came home with my box of goodies and couldn't believe what I had achieved that day.

To me, baking is like magic. It is a process of creation. I strongly believe that being actively involved in the kitchen at a young age helped me develop the personality traits that I have today. Baking teaches you patience and it teaches you precision and perfection. Recipes need to be followed to a get a flawless product. I also love thinking about how the recipe works. You should do the same. Understand the basic chemistry of your ingredients. Learn the rules so that you can modify them to fit your needs according to you what you have in your kitchen and what you like.

Working in the kitchen and creating new goodies helps me think, it helped me grow and it is the best stress buster I could ask for. Working with your hands tends to do that. I would encourage you to get your hands dirty, have fun, don't worry about what can go wrong but enjoy the process instead.

Share whatever you create and don't forget to apply what you learn in the kitchen to your life outside it. Dream as big as you can and have faith in yourself and the preparation process.

Here is a fun recipe you can try with a friend or your parents.

Jam Thumbprint Cookies

(Makes 20 medium-sized cookies)

You'll need:

- 100g butter
- 120g castor sugar
- 1 tsp vanilla essence

- 1 egg
- ½ tsp baking powder
- 175g flour
- 50g jam (any flavour of your choice)

The Baking Process:

1. Whisk butter, castor sugar and vanilla essence together until the mixture is light and fluffy.
2. Add the egg and whisk again.
3. Sift together the baking powder and flour and fold into the mixture created above with the help of a spatula
4. Mix and mix until you have dough.
5. Refrigerate it for 2 hours.
6. Preheat the oven to 165°C and line your baking tray with parchment paper.
7. Take small quantities of the dough and make small balls. Flatten them with your fingertips into medium-sized cookies.
8. Put them on the baking tray, leaving a 2-inch gap between each cookie.
9. Using your thumb, make small wells in the middle of each cookie.
10. Put a teaspoon of jam in each well.
11. Bake for 15 minutes or till the edges start browning.
12. Once cooled, top the wells with some more jam and serve.

Enjoy your own creation!

Chapter 12

Discovering Your Inner Compassion

Teens can inherit compassionate attitudes that last a lifetime. Parents and teachers can introduce her to the underprivileged and the homeless who are looking for nothing else but warmth and a meal. When a girl grows up with parents who support a cause or various causes, she learns the significance of doing her bit for others. Whether she joins you on your visits to feed the local stray dogs or she helps you put together old clothes for the poor, compassion is a trait that can catch on early if children are taught to look beyond themselves.

Schools do a good job when they organise programs to bring the students together for a charitable cause or to build awareness. Try an annual visit to the bird sanctuary or the local nature club. Go serve meals at an old age home or nursing home. Knock on your neighbours' doors to collect thing that can help the poor. There's a lot that can be done and compassion is the reason behind positive change in the world.

When you log onto news websites, you will see lots of bad news about murder, terrorism, accidents and poaching.

But if you look carefully, you will find stories about a man or woman who saved a pregnant whale from dying and helped her delivery process. Look a bit closer and you'll find a story about a person who built an entire road because his village had no access to the rest of the state. Compassion is the driving force for happiness.

It is unfortunate that empathy – the ability to feel what somebody else is feeling – is nearly dead. When you are a teenager, being happy is all about owning the latest devices, clothes and top brands. Children are mean to other children when they don't look the prescribed way or have what according to popular opinion at school is a must have. You understand how unhealthy it is to value people based on their looks and if they have an Apple iPod or a nameless music player. Entitlement is what seems to matter to most teens.

Today's girls are more used to getting material goods that they don't need and merely want. When children are judging each other according to what they have, it is hard to imagine them being sensitive to the feelings of those who own nothing or close to nothing. Since your daughter is living in that kind of environment every day, it is up to you to bring out her inner compassion at home.

You may wish take her to Singapore or Europe for vacation and give her a nice tablet and mobile phone every year. Take her out shopping every month too. Of course parents don't always do these things to spoil their daughters. Being well-rounded and having exposure to as much as possible is great but just throw compassion into the mix. Nobody will like a selfish self-obsessed teen who would probably grow up into a self-obsessed adult.

Researchers have shared their tips for raising a compassionate, responsible child. They believe that assigning chores teaches her to understand the concept of each family member taking on a specific job for the benefit of the whole family. This can entail older siblings taking care of younger siblings when the parents are out or your daughter feeding the pet one meal daily.

When you praise your daughter for doing something well, research suggests that you mention her inner characteristics within the praise. For instance, don't just say, "Thanks for making me the grocery list today. It was kind of you to understand that mom is sick." Using the word 'kind' focuses on her compassionate nature which she needs to be aware of. Don't give rewards to her whenever she does something good.

Instead, praise her and reward her occasionally because she shouldn't get the message that all work is done for rewards. As she grows older, she will realise that doing good things isn't always about getting something. Just as the dog you feed on the street won't hand you a reward in return unless you consider a happy lick and tail wag a gift. The same holds true for the beggar on the sidewalk who won't have anything to give her in return but silent gratitude.

Be open with emotions in your family. A lot of families like to keep negative emotions unexpressed. Sometimes that is how the family members have always been. At other times, it may be that strong emotional exchanges make a member uncomfortable. But research has shown that children, who are more in touch with their emotions from a young age, often have more empathy as they are used to considering and understanding people's feelings. The average teen would take feelings for granted but your daughter would not. So spend time with her and don't stay clammed up when you're upset, angry or happy either.

Last but not least, help her find places to volunteer. Researchers have found that volunteering experience is linked to increased adolescent self esteem, self acceptance and moral development. It also increases the teen's belief that it is her personal responsibility to help others. Devoting time at an animal shelter or a sick people's home can reinforce the truth that she has a lot compared to others. Then screaming and slamming doors for a tube of lip gloss won't seem like a nice thing to do.

Empathy and compassion don't happen in one day. They take time to develop. Be there to demonstrate compassion to her but don't force her to be a part of something that she doesn't care much more. Give her time to find her cause. Even if she gets emotionally hurt along the way, she will realise the value of kindness and why people should not let negative people affect their peace and positivity.

Rimi B. Chatterjee's Story

13

At the age of thirteen I discovered demons, or rather they discovered me. You know what demons are, right? I'm talking about the little voices in your head that whisper to you. They try to scare you about failure and loneliness. These demons try to convince you that you are going to fail anyway, so why bother trying to do anything in the first place? You find yourself wondering if it's really worth it to get deep into whatever it is that you're bent on doing.

These demons are very persistent. In fact, some of them will be heard from the heads of people around you. First, you'll hear small echoes under the words the person says. Basically, strain your ears to be extra intelligent because the way words are said can change everything.

Watch out for kindness with heat in it, like when your best friend's mother said, 'She's like a dog, comes whenever my daughter calls.' Or the class mate who 'lost' your best essay. You know there's logic to these things. Demons are never convincing when they smile.

Well, the good news is that there's good fighting the evil. I am talking about your guardian angels: the people who really want you to be happy. Their hearts talk too. So there are the demons and the angels speaking at the same time.

Your head must feel like exploding sometimes when they get too loud. You can't hear things clearly because there are too many people's words moving around your head. It's not your fault. When you're thirteen, other people just have to be your guardian angels. If they do their jobs well and guide you to happiness and success, they can teach you how to take the guardian out of their heads and put it where it belongs - in your head, of course.

Your network of guardian angels consisting of parents, teachers, and mentors try to accomplish this by saying, get up, go get dressed, go to school, stand up to that bully, run away from that fake friend, and love that good person. If they do this wrong, or do it badly, then you end up with an infected protector. Its sickness is that it protects itself at the expense of others, and eventually itself. So you find yourself throwing that sweet wrapper out the window instead of the bin. .Being nice to the school bully, choosing the career your parents want you to have, giving up your dreams because dreams can't be trusted.

Ok now here's the hard part. You need the demons. If you don't let them in and hear what they have to say, you'll never learn to fight them. Actually I don't need to tell you this, because I know you'll never be able to fight the voice that says 'Help me!' Even if it's a trap laid by a person who's just taking advantage of your weakness, you will listen.

You see, it is not enough to always be good on your own. Sure, you can keep your mouth shut and stay out of trouble just fine. But you can't avoid other people forever. One of them will walk up to you and shake your hand someday. What will you do then, run away? You can't run forever. So here's the deal.

Firstly- and you're going to give me an odd look when I say this- there is just one love. All real love is one. It is undividable. If you love something truly, something else you love truly cannot demand that you sacrifice the first thing to it. If this does happen, then one of the loves is wrong. Figure out which one is a demon and dump it. Okay, that may sound impossible to get into your young brain, so let me try to break down this whole thing about compassion.

You're going to go through life connecting (and disconnecting) with things and people you love. Everyone who isn't living in a cave does that. If you are smart, you'll collect things and people that go together because you don't want craziness. You think, "But what if I like people and things that don't go together?" That's a perfectly reasonable question, but the truth is that you will only like things and people that don't go together if you are divided within yourself. I see you frowning. You don't like this restriction upon your choices. But think for a while.

The reason you like these people is that they too are divided within themselves as you are; they too are facing a war of sorts within their minds. What they want to do is part positive and part negative. Their thoughts are a mix of good and bad. The positive angel parts may be very beautiful indeed but that doesn't matter. If the demons are powerful enough, they will eat up the angel. If you try to save it, you'll be lunch too. Be careful.

Deal with this situation. Get smart. Listen to what both the demon and the angel tell you. Don't tune out the negative energy when it talks. When it talks, get your sword out. I mean, pick holes in whatever it says. Don't let it do your thinking for you, or wear you down, or change the subject. Also, do not let it bore you into agreeing that wrong is right. If it bangs the door and leaves, fine, let it go. Demons hate intelligence. That's why the demons in your head and in other people's heads will constantly try to make you think that you're stupid. Throw your weapon at it - common sense. Every time you start to doubt yourself or what you're doing because of these negative, nasty thoughts, use your common sense.

You need to stop the angel part from leaving as well, so talk and listen to it too. Tell it about gentleness. Tell it about compassion. Gentleness is a combination of peace and love. Compassion is the end of suffering. If you have both of these, you can make a difference in this world and in many lives. It's quite simple. Every time the demon does something, look the angel in the eye and say, "You should be ashamed." Remember to look the angel in the eye, not the demon, because demons have no shame.

Imagine the angel-face you want to see peeping out, and speak to it. If it sticks its tongue out, or throws stones at you, get out of the way. Look for those who need your kindness.

It's the ones you want to save that will give you the most trouble. They will behave just as badly, but the difference is, after you kill their demon they will come back and try to behave better. There may be no other encouraging signs at all. You will have to decide whether you want to accept the challenge or not. Believe me when I say that the wrong choice can lead to a mess. So getting good at picking the ones who can be saved is a major survival skill. Unfortunately, only trial and error and your own guardian angel can help you with that.

I'm not your guardian angel; I'm you from thirty years into the future. While you are confused about dealing with people right now, I have learned and relearned everything that there is to know. Anyway, let's suppose you decide the person you're helping is worth fighting for. The first thing you do is observe them and figure out which of their actions belongs to the angel and which to the demons.

You see, the demons are all the results of past wounds. Think about it this way: If a girl was always called ugly by that nasty voice in her head, she will be quite sensitive about her appearance. When you say something nice to her about how she looks one day, she will reply with bitterness and suspicion. Why? Because she'll think that you're lying, you must be, and that makes you a bad person. Understand now? It's not about you at all. So the demon is like a cat stuck in a tree, too scared to come down, but ready to scratch a rescuing hand. As long as it's using its cat brain, you're going to be looking for band aids, but if you can get the human brain to wake up and pay attention, then there is hope. Therefore, talk to such a person carefully. Put yourself in her shoes.

You're fidgeting. You don't want to do this? Well, you won't have a choice. You see, people know what you are. They know what you can do, it's like they can smell it. All the lost ones will be drawn to you. It's like a curse. But you can't do anything about it. You were born that way, and ever since you can remember, you've been looking at people and seeing their tears and thinking they were your own. Dry your eyes. There's work to do. You'll help and help and be exhausted. You'll help and fail sometimes. People will drain you out until you can teach this skill to the others around you. This is a time when the demon slayers are needed more than ever. Yes, you need to beat the negative people, the negative thoughts, and the negative actions around you and in yourself. And thirteen is a time when people like you are stopped before they start, when they're too young to fight. At a time in your lives when just a drop of love would turn you to the light, all you see is darkness.

That place is called the abyss. It's where you go when you don't know. You've seen it in visions and nightmares: it's where you end up when your question seems to have no answer. You know the place where you ask yourself questions like: Why do people do this? How do I make them stop? How do I stop feeling beaten up? When you ask these questions, you are wandering in the desert that lies between the world of matter and that of mind.

The first thing you do is, you find a mental camel to ride, right? Yes, pretend to be a camel. Camels can get by on very little, so you learn to live alone and take care of yourself. The second step is all about habit. Habit is incredibly powerful. It can get you out of bed and into work on days when you feel like breathing is too much work. Habit makes you run on rails. Polish your rails up with regular journeys, even if you can't go much above walking speed. The next step is to cry yourself a river and swim across when your rails drown. Building a boat's good too, because then you can pull other people in when they need help. And finally, when you become your own guardian angel, you grow wings, and then the abyss doesn't matter to you anymore. It'll just be the forgettable hole where you drop the demons after you defeat them.

Look after your body and learn to fight. At the most brutal level, the demons will want to try their strength, and make no mistake, they won't be merciful unless you beat them. If you lose, the negative energies will infect you with their ways and pains, and you will lose your positivity. But if you can crush the demons without doing a single wrong thing, then when the demons are defeated and lying flat on the floor, they will crawl away and never trouble you again.

One more thing. I know that like all kids, when you hear or read of fairytales about people getting to make magic wishes, you like to spend a lazy hour or so wondering what you would choose. Maybe a magical sword that cuts at a distance? A cup that never gets empty? A broomstick? But I know now what you would have wished for, if a genie had really showed up one night and given you the chance to make a wish. You should have chosen the power to do always what you should.

But will is something that even a powerful genie can't grant you. No one can give you will. Only you can.

Basically, the first step to do anything is to tell yourself a story about yourself. Make the story as convincing, as believable, as it-could-really-happen as you can, using all your skills of plot and character, and then you go out there and make it real. Be the person you want to be, in the story that you want for yourself. In other words, only you can believe in yourself. Kill off the doubts and stop letting any demons get to you. That's how anyone changes the world.

Keep at it and one day you will tell a story that will have the worst demons crushed to the ground. Keep your sword sharp for that day, and teach all your friends to use theirs too. You have an advantage over the demon: you can use your good to build loyalty and trust in the people you help. That's your superpower. You can make your friends and the world like you by giving them love and teaching them to give love too. All the hard work you did killing off the demons will pay off then.

That's all I wanted to say. I suspect you'll go ahead and make the mistakes. You will take the wrong turns. Demons will make life suck sometimes. If all that didn't happen, I wouldn't be sharing all this. But don't worry. Even in the darkest depths of the deep, dark hole, you will have an advantage: you know how the story ends.

Chapter 13

Terrible Tantrums!

A thirteen-year-old girl is never going to like the word 'no'. Accepting a no from her parents will be difficult, but it is bound to happen during this time when she sees popularity as a bigger goal than being reasonable. A rebellious streak is nothing out of the ordinary under such circumstances. Actually, rebellion is necessary to help her find her own identity and realise what is most important to her. Experts look at it as a process that ends with the teenager defining herself as a unique person, separate from her parents. So after all those years of being sheltered and lead by the hand at every step, your child needs to develop. This makes tantrums seem more positive, doesn't it?

Understandably, you won't feel that way when you're facing the rage of your teen. She will scream at you and say that she hates you. She will slam her door and stay locked in her room for hours. Her temper tantrums can leave every family member miserable as if she is spreading the bitterness that she is feeling. Sometimes you may think you are a bad parent for disliking your own daughter so much as she wreaks havoc through the house. There will be episodes about dating, boys, going out to meet friends, staying out late and even about her wardrobe. Then there will be the demands for tablets, shopping trips to the biggest brand name stores. Most of the time, her list of wants will be generated from what her peers are talking about and buying.

It won't be easy, but try your best to listen to her after she calms down. Hear her out. That doesn't mean that you have to change your stance on the subject. It just gives her the comfort of knowing that you aren't turning down her demands without giving her a chance to share her point of view. She is really sensitive right now with all the physical, emotional and social changes going on in her life, so don't ignore her anxiety. She needs you even though she doesn't say so. In fact, she needs you more than before because you are the ones who are going to be at the receiving end of most of her temper tantrums. Funny thought, right?

Your daughter is on the search for maximum personal control or independence from you. Her reactions to the disagreements that occur between you are a natural reaction because she sees you as the person who wants to ruin her fun and make her unpopular. Picture an incident where your daughter has come home wearing a friend's expensive watch. Most parents would not like to see this. Imagine that you tell her, "You should not have taken her watch."

She will not understand why you are upset. Then when you tell her to return the watch in school the next day, she may start screaming and throwing a tantrum because she sees this instruction from you as a desire to ruin her friendship with the girl who gave her the watch. At an age when friends are more important than anyone else in the world, this assumption can elicit in an intense response from her. If you wait for her to finish ranting, crying and shouting back, you may be able to sit with her and explain to her why she should not take anything that a friend gives her.

While researchers, doctors and parents have blamed the 'raging hormones' for the Terrible Teens, they are not the only reason for rampant emotions manifesting themselves. In recent times, new research on brain development has shown that along with hormones, the brain is responsible for how your teenager thinks and behaves.

David Walsh, president and founder of the National Institute of Media and the Family in Minneapolis (USA) believes that even though parents think their children are misinterpreting situations or trying to drive them crazy on purpose, this is not true. This psychologist says that the tantrums and moody behaviour are the result of a teen's prefrontal cortex which is the brain's centre for moderation, impulse-control and the understanding of outcomes still being under construction, added to the surging hormones.

Since the formation of this area is not completed yet, impulsive behaviour and quick anger occurs. Researchers at a leading United States university have found links between discipline and good teaching. These professors and researchers at Brigham Young University think that using a proactive teaching approach to discipline can be applied to dealing with tantrums with children of all ages, including teenagers. They outlined three steps to guide parents.

The first step is to review the risks. This encompasses all the personal risks that come up while you are dealing with a reactive teenager. During this time, you need to think twice before you reprimand your daughter for throwing a tantrum directed at you even though she is the one at fault after losing her new mobile phone. But can your reaction to her behaviour start a worse stream of incidents to disrupt the family?

Find a way that works for you so that you can maintain your cool in these situations. The second step is to consider how you can create a positive, safe environment for your daughter. Reinforcing her confidence with praise, love and support keeps everybody happy. So then assigning the occasional punishment on her won't seem like extreme behaviour to her. Finally, parents need to think of themselves as teachers. Talk to your teen calmly, in a tone that would earn you her respect so that she can respond without a major tantrum even if there is a disagreement between the two of you

There are of course, cultural differences in the methods used to deal with unruly teenage behaviour. Popular opinion can range from reprimanding parents who administer the occasional slap to praising those parents who give regular physical punishment. It depends on the people of your region. But sometimes a good shaking up is all that is needed when things seem to be going out of control. Above all, your daughter should not forget that you are her guide, support system and that you will always look out for her best interests.

Sheena Misra Ghosh's Story

13

I was one of those vivacious, constantly bubbly, giggling little girls. As I approached thirteen, I was made to feel quite special with loads of celebration and mental tutoring which was done so gently and subtly that I only realise it in hindsight. All this and more was done by not merely my parents, but the larger extended family. There was my very special aunt, my paternal as well as maternal grandparents and my cousins and sisters even though they were younger than me. We all felt that something big was going to happen. We understood that a phase that would last till nineteen ended was about to start. Surely there was something big about this row of years all ending with 'teen'.

A lot of things were experienced in those years. I recall feeling conscious of my physical appearance. My flat-chest, my bow-legged lower body and my freckles; none of it appealed to my peers and they would tease me. Fortunately for me, my parents knew how to make me feel better so my confidence was not deflated. They told me that my chest, legs and freckles were just like those possessed by people in the western world.

They said that the girls in those countries have skinny, athletic figures and very sensitive skin, so they have freckles.

According to my parents, I had been born of that origin but got displaced by mistake. That episode taught me a parenting technique that I recommend to all other parents. Peer criticism can cause a lot of pain when the girls are trying too hard to be liked. Unconditional love from you can guide her to unconditional acceptance of things that make her unhappy.

While I was still in my teens, my parents realized that I was a total failure as far as household chores and kitchen work was concerned. Unlike most kids who are enthusiastic about helping their moms in the kitchen, I was a disaster and was never enthusiastic about doing any housework because I was scared of being ridiculed.

You see, my two younger sisters were so adept at it that I feared comparison, although my parents never let sibling rivalry become an issue. My father promptly developed a strategy which would not only save my face but also help my confidence. One day when we had guests visiting us for dinner, he told the guests that all the food was made with the help of one of his younger twin daughters, while the table and room were neatly arranged by the other twin, and since I was good at socialising and loved being with people, I would be taking care of the guests by chatting with them.

This is one parental strategy I place above all else as a psychologist. Since thirteen and its surrounding years are a phase of social awkwardness and self consciousness, teenagers may shy away from taking responsibility because failing may result in a humiliating situation. Criticism and reprimands by parents are important but so is being sensitive because hypersensitivity is yet another characteristic of these years.

This means that your daughter can shock you by oscillating between intense anger and being extremely sensitive and bursting into tears. . This sort of behaviour comes from her confusion and frustration while she tries to figure out who she is and what she is supposed to be like. So I am thankful that my parents not only praised me but also made to feel on top of the world as they found my strengths and did not make me feel bad about my weaknesses.

When it came to the big decision of choosing my career, my parents stood by me once again. While most of my friends were trying to live up to the parental expectations and societal pressures by taking up science and commerce subjects, I was subtly encouraged to try out off beat, yet futuristic subjects like psychology.

My parents helped me find a lot of information regarding the application of psychology in various fields and areas of our lives. I read about psychology being used in the corporate world. I read about it being applied to help children. I was amazed to see how the study of human behaviour and the human mind could be associated with everything. I immediately felt like I was studying the most happening subject of the decade and my self confidence soared high.

Gadgets are constantly upgraded and these teens are well-versed with the constant changes. For example, she may demand that you buy her a new mobile phone immediately even though her current one serves her purpose of calling home when out with friends and playing games and chatting with friends. If you say no, she can scream and shout and throw a tantrum that lasts for days. She can also resort to manipulative behavior by not agreeing to eat her meals or shutting herself up in a room when guests are invited to the house

She thinks that acting like this will make her win her unreasonable demand. She may even lay down conditions saying, "I will get 90 per cent marks if you give me the phone." Instead of trying to respond with a logical explanation or finding a way out of the unpleasant situation, parents should tell her the truth. Tell her that you cannot afford what she wants right now or that she cannot have a new mobile phone every few months.

Today, children are asking for things that they have done no research on. They see it so they want it. Ask them questions about the product they want you do buy. Gauge if they are genuinely interested. Then ask them "Do you really need it?" Remember that you are dealing with a person who is operating on what we psychologists call the Pleasure Principle. This means that she only wants immediate pleasure and no pain. But as she grows older, she will realise that all pleasure doesn't come instantly. She will find out through her teenage experiences that there is such a thing as earning what you want or facing obstacles to achieve or acquire what you want. On the other hand, if a girl's parents give her whatever she asks for, whenever she asks; it will be hard for her to learn about the way life works.

Even then, things won't be easy for your daughter because she will feel like she isn't living up to the standard of her peers. At thirteen, the exterior is more important than the substance. As in the case of the phone where she doesn't really need one but believes she has to have one. Same thing when it comes to her peers as she admires the ones who seem most confident and attractive in appearance. But parents and teachers need to be alert for teen tantrum problems. If the frequency of tantrums is increasing or if trivial matters are turning into harmful actions, a professional needs to intervene. For instance, if your daughter is harming others to try to get her demands met, or lying to you, you should worry. Say, for example, if she throws away her father's phone just because she is not getting a new one for herself.

Be careful because there is a thin line between temper

tantrums and emerging mental illness. In fact, the onset of many psychological problems happens during the teenage years. Disorders such as mood disorder and borderline personality disorder can show their first signs. And girls have a strong tendency to be victims of borderline personality disorder. Symptoms of this disorder include marked mood swings, inappropriate intense anger; self-harming behaviour, fear of being abandoned, feeling empty or bored, and rocky relationships with people and seeing life as all good or all bad.

Don't let this kind of behaviour go unnoticed. It is best not to argue with them at this time. Be a patient listener at first. Being heard makes a whole lot of difference to teens, which ultimately makes them feel accepted. Also give them the time to think over the issue and work it out in their own minds and they may soon see logic. Teenagers need to be dealt with gently but firmly. As soon as they are made to face the consequences of their action they get their act together. Try to look for the feeling behind the tantrum and not just the tantrum on the surface.

Take on the challenging teenage phase and keep in mind that parenting is all about being you. An adult does not need to get completely psyched out of his or her mind to learn the different chapters of Parenting. Rather, deal with each issue intuitively, spontaneously and empathetically. The more trusting and open parents are in their own styles of living and managing themselves, the better cues girls will pick up on how to act, behave and manage themselves. So do not be afraid of failing to learn parenting skills. Thirteen and the teens can be a splendid phase so learn to accept your girls as they are. Enjoy your time with them and guide them to success.

Chapter 14

Surviving Child Sexual Abuse

India is no stranger to teen sexual abuse. Sadly, it is too familiar with incidents of rape and molestation lately. The victims cover every age group, horrifyingly starting from a few months old to older women. The famous Nirbhaya rape case in Delhi acted as an eye opener to a frequent act of injustice and trauma that most people ignore. It isn't like the newspapers and TV media are reporting every case though because sexual abuse victims face social stigma that stops them from taking any action at all.

Then there is the alarming statistic from Indian Police records that says that in more than 90 per cent of the cases of sexual violence, the offenders are people whom the victim knows. So the challenge is not just about making sure that your daughter is alright when she is outside her house, since even relatives can be involved in such acts. You would assume that being indoors with family and extended family was the safest she could be, but thinking that way has affected the lives of many young sexual abuse victims. Research shows that often the perpetrator of a sexual crime is someone who is known to the victim, and may even be a male family member.

A girl would certainly doubt that her parents would believe her if she said that an uncle was behaving inappropriately with her when they were alone. Worse still, a young girl may not even be sure that what is happening to her can be called sexual abuse. At the extreme end of the scale, sexual abuse includes sexual intercourse. But all offences that involve sexually touching a child, as well as non-touching offences and sexual exploitation, are just as harmful and devastating to a child's well-being. That basically means that you need to teach her the difference between a pat on the back versus a back rub with sexual intentions. You need to tell her that a parent kissing her on the cheek is different from somebody else doing it.

The good news is that there are organisations and people who are actively working towards an India where children (and adult) victims will not be scared to speak out. One of these community development organisations is called Plan India. At Plan India, they protect children and all youth from violence of any form. They also fight against gender discrimination that is prevalent through the culture. Issues of child marriage, abuse for dowry and the gender gap in education are a reflection of what many citizens in India believe in. One of Plan India's campaigns called The Chuppi Todo (Break the silence) campaign against child sexual abuse, commenced in Delhi in 2010.

Through this movement, they teach school children about Good Touch versus Bad Touch and explain to them why they should report sexual abuse to the authorities. In the same year, the organization carried out a survey of 10000 girls in Ten Indian Cities. Across the different cities, more than 77 per cent of the participants reported sexual harassment or eve teasing, as the term is used, as one of the biggest disadvantages in the city. That is a big number.

So you need to be cautious and let your daughter know that sexual abuse and harassment are things that she may face. Then tell her what to do if she encounters such behaviour. Discussions about sex and sexuality are treated as a taboo topic in most schools and homes. Once you create such an aura of mystery and negativity around something, you can expect your teen to shy away from asking you questions or revealing anything to you. Don't avoid her queries or tell her that she is too young to know about these things. She isn't. You know that her body is changing and very important to her now because she wants to look her best and impress the boys and feel confident amongst her peers. You also know very well that her body is capable of new experiences after puberty hits. So why leave her in a lurch without any information and guidance?

Instead, teach your daughter to come and talk to you if she feels that she has been violated in some way. Tell her that unwanted touching happens but it is never her fault. She needs to share it with you whether it happens at school, or at home or on a train. Don't use nicknames for body parts when you are explaining things to her.

Some parents devise silly names for breasts, penis and vagina, possibly thinking that saying these names out loud in front of their little girls will be harmful. But it really is better than leaving her in the dark because then she may find herself unable to discuss sex related issues with you later on and if and when sexual abuse takes place. Admittedly, she won't be a complete stranger to these matters with a plethora of images and data on the internet, but it is better that she hears it from you. Keep the channels of communication open for your daughter

In the event that your daughter is sexually abused, you must believe her when she discloses the details to you – even if the offender is somebody you used to trust. Nothing can justify sexual abuse of a child. Don't make the mistake of trying to find excuses for the person who has committed such an act. That would just make your daughter feel all alone and guilty. She has come to you for help.

Don't ask her for details immediately; let her share however much or little she is ready to reveal at first. When you do ask her questions, be careful with your choice of words. "Why did he touch you?" That is a question that justifies her abuse. Or asking her what she was wearing is another way to add to her distress. The debate on clothes being the reason for a girl's rape or molestation has been on for a long time. But isn't it clear that girls in salwar kameezes are as vulnerable as those who wear jeans or skirts?

Talk to her but remember that one conversation won't be enough. Get assistance from mental health practitioners who can join you in being her support system. And last of all, the ramifications of sexual abuse last for a lifetime but that doesn't mean that you can't help her heal.

Pranaadhika Sinha Devburman's Story

13

Back in the day when I was a somewhat sprightly 13-year old, fielding various challenges and celebrating a few triumphs, life could be best described as being rather average. There were no "adult" responsibilities to speak of, and yet there were these little burdens on the soul, which added up, and sometimes made me feel like I was the only teenager in the world (well, in the neighbourhood at least) who had the weight of the universe on her shoulders.

Weight gain, hormones, pimples, sexual abuse, crushes on boys, being crushed on by boys, constant fights with my mother, missing my father and wondering why we couldn't live in the same house; the problems were at times, endless. And yet, at times, it seemed as if everything was going to be okay. Looking back, I feel that peer group support and heart-to-heart conversations with my mother helped smoothen the aforementioned bumps in my personal road towards adulthood. I also made it a point to maintain a journal from age 9, which facilitated the all-important "venting" process, or else there's a lot that suppressed emotion can do which could ruin the rest of your life, not to mention your relationships, or even your career when you have one.

One of the more traumatic experiences in my young life,

which I believe has shaped me in a considerable manner, involved multiple experiences with childhood sexual abuse, incest, and rape. They started when I was four years old, and stopped when I was about nineteen. From a trusted relative who shall not be named, to a trusted servant, to various other abusers, the common thread that connected them all was the fact that they were "trusted" people, i.e. they belonged to that "safe" category that we create for people whom we feel have the credibility and the wherewithal to take care of our loved ones and keep them safe.

A number of studies in India and abroad have proved that over 80 per cent of perpetrators of sex offenders are someone who the child knows and trusts; this automatically indicates that they are a part of the aforementioned "safe" category. Given that I am living proof of the safe category being rather unsafe, it would be wise for parents to keep an open mind and an open door with regard to the possibility that their child 'might' be abused by a trusted person. Please do not disbelieve or shut your child out in the event that they come to you for help, and tell you that the abuser is someone you know, trust, or are related to by blood. Abuse within families where the abuser is a family member, is very common; the popular film *Monsoon Wedding* highlighted this most effectively.

In many cases where I have counseled families whose children have been abused, the common argument has been "but he/she (the abuser) has known us for years and they come from a good family. They also have kids of their own, so how can they be capable of abusing my child?" The truth is that there is no specific way to differentiate between an abusive person from a non-abusive person, and factors pertaining to their apparently "good", socially acceptable backgrounds have nothing to do with the thoughts in their heads. Please note that I mentioned both "he" as well as "she" while referring to abusers; this is because both men and women are equally capable of being vulnerable to abuse, and they are also equally capable of carrying out an act of abuse.

A little online search should clear any doubts in this area, since the media has been doing an exceptional job at highlighting cases of abuse and incest around the world. Another point I would like to make with regard to "good people from good families" is that we need to stop labeling things randomly; good and bad are firstly, very subjective terms. Secondly, just because a person is rich, has a car, and outwardly, seems to be living the perfect life, does not make them a "good" human being; of course it does not make them bad either. Everyone, regardless of his or her religion, bank balance, caste or creed, can be an abuser. Just because you call them Uncle or Bhaiya or Aunty, does not guarantee that they are incapable of hurting you. The famous saying, "with great power comes great responsibility" applies here, and as parents, it is important for you to explain these facts of life to your child in a manner, which does not scare them.

The objective is to let your child know that you, the parent, love them and will listen to them and will "believe" them. Not believing a child, or reacting badly to abuse, is what has led to so many young survivors of abuse shutting up from within and refusing to share, thereby shutting off their chances of healing from the trauma of abuse.

Getting down to definitions in order to understand what constitutes sexual abuse, and understanding the short and long-term implications of it, will help parents and children develop an action plan pertaining to discussion, disclosure and healing.

> "*Sexual abuse includes any situation in which children are being used for someone else's sexual gratification,*

ranging from hands-on abuse, such as fondling, oral sex, or intercourse, to exposure to disturbing sexual material. Sexual abuse can be traumatic to children since it is an overwhelming, out of the ordinary experience, and elicits feelings of helplessness and instinctual arousal."

—Eliana Gil, Ph.D.

The following are some of the most common signs or symptoms of child sexual abuse:

- acting out sexual behaviour
- inappropriate interest or knowledge of sexual acts and language
- excessive touching of genitals
- sexually transmitted diseases (STDs) or urinary infections
- chronic stomach aches, vomiting
- an abrupt change in personality or behaviour
- nightmares, bed-wetting
- drastic change in appetite
- self-mutilation
- withdrawal/depression
- regressive behaviour such as thumb-sucking
- consistently anxious, fearful, irritable
- reluctance to be with a particular person or in a particular place
- over compliance
- elective mutism
- excessive aggression (particularly in boys)
- running away, stealing, lying
- early arrival at school or reluctance to go home
- early use of drugs or alcohol

Additional Signs May Be Present In Older Children

- drug and alcohol use
- delinquency
- running away
- depression
- early sexual involvement
- promiscuity
- suicide attempts
- eating disorders (anorexia/bulimia)

[List courtesy – Mansi Goenka, CSA Survivor]

What to do if you or someone you know has been or is being abused –

The first thing to do is to ensure that you/the survivor is in a safe place, i.e. away from the abuser physically. If not, get out of the unsafe place and find a safe space away from them, ideally a public place or with a trusted person (we will discuss "trusted person" in detail later).

The second thing is to listen. Do not panic or begin expressing your personal thoughts about the abuser or the survivor. This is the time to be quiet and allow the survivor the space to share or remain quiet; the choice is theirs. You must understand that it is important to give power back to the survivor by allowing them control over the situation. Do not force them to talk, and if they do, allow them to continue for as long as they wish to.

The third thing is to Empathise. Do not play moral police – that is the last thing the survivor needs. It does not matter what they were wearing or what they said. No child is responsible for a sexually abusive act and judging them or passing silly statements amounts to re-victimisation of an already traumatised individual.

The fourth thing to do, in the event that you too, are a minor, is to seek professional intervention for the survivor. This is very important and requires a lot of thought, since for example, many cases of abuse involve incest or abuse by a family member. In these cases it may or may not be a good idea to approach the survivor's family, since responses can vary from disbelief to hostility. A teacher could help, or in some cases, various children's help lines and NGOs can also come forward as impartial mediators.

The final thing to do as a parent, or as someone who is handling the disclosure, is to ensure that the survivor is comfortable at all times, and is allowed to make decisions which should be respected, regardless of whether you agree with them or not. For example, if the survivor does not want to file a police complaint, it is their choice. However some exceptions should be made in the case of rape, where medical attention is mandatory in order to prevent infections and further issues.

Dealing with the disclosure of sexual abuse is of primary importance. The reason as to why so many people are silent about sexual abuse, only to reveal their experiences during adulthood, is because they were either afraid to talk about it, or because their disclosures were met with negative reactions. As mentioned, the 4 things to do will guide a person as to how to manage a situation without causing further trauma to the survivor. It is now time to share some safe statements, which can be made during the disclosure process in order to provide comfort and encouragement to the survivor.

"*I am here for you if you would like to talk about it, and need someone to listen.*"

"*What you tell me will remain between us, this is your pain, and only you have the right to share or not share it with other people.*"

"This was not your fault at all, I am on your side. Let me know if I can help you find a doctor/trusted person/teacher who can guide you on what to do."

Adolescence is like the proverbial rollercoaster ride, and with sexual awakening and hormones, come a number of revelations about life, people, and the world at large. Revelations and realisations pertaining to sexual abuse and incest need to be dealt with the utmost sensitivity and care, or else they will negatively impact the long-term growth of the child. Speaking from personal experience, I grew up to be an intelligent and perceptive young girl who hated herself for reasons unknown, and never took part in competitive activities because she did not think she was good enough to win. Self-harming is common among young people as are suicidal tendencies, and contrary to what one would like to believe; very few of these behaviours have anything to do with a poor academic performance or a fight with a boyfriend or girlfriend.

Many times the kinds of behaviour which we would like to think are attributed to "normal" aspects of growing up are actually the person's way of displaying conscious or subconscious trauma. Regular and open communication with your child, letting them know that you are on their side no matter what, and believing them when they share a terrible secret with you, will all contribute towards the positive healing process which, while it does not erase the abuse entirely, will certainly reduce the scars of it.

Who's Who

Anjali Raina is the Executive Director of the Harvard Business School (HBS) India Research Centre (IRC). Prior to joining HBS IRC Anjali spent 15 years with Citigroup India, most recently as Country Director, before which she worked for more than a decade with ANZ Grindlays Bank PLC. Anjali holds an MBA from the Indian Institute of Management, Calcutta, a bachelor's degree from Loreto College and is an alumnus of HBS having completed the Advanced Management Program. Under her leadership, the HBS IRC has facilitated the writing of over 155 case studies on Indian Business Practice and supported half a dozen research projects. Anjali has co-authored several case studies. She is also a Director on the Board of Harvard Business Publishing, India, the Regional President (Western Region) of NHRDN, an Advisor to The Akanksha Foundation, Trustee to LIFE Trust, an Advisory Member on the Board of HBS Club of India, and on the Advisory Board of the Indian Business School.

Anjali Sharma enrolled as an Advocate in 1988. She is practicing law as a senior associate in a New Delhi based law firm called Integral Law Offices. The firm does extensive work in the commercial, corporate, contract, and arbitration law fields. Anjali is a litigation lawyer, with considerable experience in documentation as well. She is also an animal rights activist, and is an executive committee member of, and legal advisor to the Animal Welfare Board of India, which is a statutory body functioning under the aegis of the Ministry of Environment and Forests.

Avantika Akerkar is the Chief Executive of Prana Worldwide, a global consultancy that specialises in transforming human potential through innovative learning and development interventions. She came to India in 2000 after spending over 15 years in the United States. Born and raised in Mumbai, Avantika returned from the US to involve herself with a consortium of NGOs dedicated to improving the civic life of the Mumbaiker. As a consultant, she worked with companies on projects such as Mumbai's first international marathon, a cross-border peace initiative between marginalised children from Pakistan and India, an international film festival, and a sustainable alternative to public transportation. She is also an acclaimed theatre actress and has acted in plays with Oscar winners Jane Fonda and Marissa Tomei, and locally, Shabana Azmi, Konkana Sen and others.

Ishi Khosla a practicing clinical nutritionist is actively involved in clinical practice at the Centre for Dietary Counselling, New Delhi. She was the Head of the Nutrition Department at the Department of Preventive Cardiology, Fortis Escorts Heart Institute and Research Centre, New Delhi, for several years and contributes to India's leading publications and newspapers including Times of India, Indian Express, Hindustan times and Prevention magazine to name a few. She lectures extensively, conducts nutrition workshops across the country and is frequently invited to radio and television programs. Ishi has also authored three books. She is on the Board of Advisors of the National Television (Doordarshan) and is also a Board member of Lady Irwin College, University of Delhi, the oldest and most prestigious institution of nutrition in the country. As part of her commitment towards community nutrition and public health, Ishi founded The Celiac Society For Delhi in 2006. She has been listed among the 25 most powerful women in the country by the India Today Group. In 2001, she founded Whole Foods India, the first health food company in India. She is also the founder of www.theweightmonitor.com.

Komal Sood is an alumnus of the National Institute of Fashion and Technology (NIFT), Kolkata, and Central Saint Martin's College of Art & Design (London). She launched her label, Kommal Sood in 2005, a label that now retails from leading stores in India and the Middle East. The label epitomises refinement and luxury in fashion. The essence of the brand is youthful, chic glamour and sophistication. The meticulously crafted ensembles are an innovative mix of Eastern suggestions and European sensibility. The distinctiveness is fluid silhouettes, defined cuts and eclectic embroidery.

Malini Agarwal is the Founder and Blogger-in-Chief of MissMalini.com. The website is India's leading celebrity lifestyle and entertainment blog. A fixture in Mumbai's entertainment scene for over 10 years, MissMalini is a regular feature in India's top fashion publications. Before the blog, Malini was a radio deejay and the co-host of a popular style-centric television show. Her website is the destination of choice for the latest celebrity news, fashion trends and styling tips from India and around the world.

Meher Pudumjee is the Chairperson of Thermax Ltd. A postgraduate in Chemical Engineering from the Imperial College of Science & Technology, London, Meher joined Thermax as a trainee engineer in 1990. A year later, along with her husband Pheroz Pudumjee and a small team, they took over the responsibility of turning around a Thermax subsidiary company in the UK. After her return to India in 1996, she was appointed on the Board of Directors. She worked closely with the treasury and working capital management functions of Thermax, and also in the Environment Divisions of the company. In 2001, the family decided to take on non-executive roles on the Board. During this period she played an active role in the turnaround of the company. She has taken over as Chairperson, Thermax Limited, effective October 5, 2004. Meher has a keen interest in music, especially western classical and is a member of a Pune based choir. She is personally involved with the NGO's Teach For India, Akanksha and Shakti Sustainable Energy Foundation. She is the proud mother of an 18-year-old son and 15-year-old daughter.

Pooja Dhingra is the founder of Le15 Pâtisserie – Times Food Guide award winner for best desserts in Mumbai – and Studio Fifteen Culinary Centre in Mumbai. A graduate of Le Cordon Bleu, Paris, she brought a piece of that world to India through her delectable desserts and cafe. She has been featured in several national dailies and is a regular in fashion and lifestyle glossies not just for her abilities in the kitchen, but also as a dynamic businesswoman and an inspiration to women.She was selected by Forbes India for their 30 under 30 entrepreneurs list and has been voted a Rising Star by GC Watches while being featured in their global campaign. The menu at Le15 Pâtisserie has been praised in several prestigious publications in India and abroad. Bollywood stars, sportspeople, corporate czars and politicians are regular clients. Recently, her book *The Big Book of Treats* was released. Written with a professional's exacting eye and a home chef's ability to improvise, it teaches the reader how to make everything from cookies and cupcakes to brownies and birthday cakes.

Pranaadhika Sinha Devburman was raised as part of a royal family in India. She survived multiple instances of child sexual abuse, from a family member, a building caretaker and a family friend. Though she spoke out about this abuse at a young age, no family member believed her story until she was 25 years old. When her parents finally acknowledged the abuses that their daughter survived – 21 years later – Pranaadhika's parents were quite literally cast out of the family. Since no support groups were available to her, Pranaadhika created her own. Thus began Elaan, Pranaadhika's personal crusade to break the culture of secrecy and create a safe place to heal. As an individual, Pranaadhika's social development work has been featured in most prominent magazines and newspapers including Femina, YOUTH, The Hindu and others. She frequently appears on television debates and news shows to speak about rape and its prevention. She also conducts self defense classes at educational institutions. In 2012, Pranaadhika received the Point of Faith Award from Drawing Hope International in Hollywood, California for her work.

Preeti Vyas is the Mumbai based founder and Chief Fun Officer of FunOKPlease Publishing India, an independent publishing house focused on creating original and contemporary Indian content for children. Preeti graduated in Physics from St. Xavier's College, Mumbai and in Retail Management from Victoria University Australia. Over her 18 year career she has had extensive experience and exposure to children's products/services and nearly all aspects of running retail businesses. She specialises in idea-creation, concept design and start-ups and has launched various new business ventures including her own children's bookstore called Kidztown in Mumbai, Depot. Preeti loves travelling, photography, cooking, reading and writing, but most of all she enjoys escaping into imaginary worlds of dragons, volcanoes and dinosaurs with her five-year-old. She lives in Mumbai with her husband Amish and son Neel.

Rashmi Uday Singh is the award winning author of 34 books, and a television host. She has many firsts her credit: India's first ever city-restaurant guide in 1997 and most recently, the world's first vegetarian guide to Paris. More than 20 years ago, Singh produced, scripted and directed and presented India's first TV Health show on DD Metro. Having studied journalism, law, management and trained with the BBC, she worked with the prestigious Indian Revenue Service, which she quit after fifteen years as Deputy Commissioner to follow her creative muse in newsprint and television. She is the jury chairperson from the Indian subcontinent of the London based Worlds 50 best restaurant Academy, the India contributing editor of Miele Restaurant guide, the Asia food guide and represents India in international forums. Her book A vegetarian in Paris has recently been awarded the World Gourmand Cookbook Award in Paris, February 2013.

Rimi B. Chatterjee is the author of three novels, *Black Light, The City of Love* and *Signal Red. The City of Love*, set in sixteenth century Bengal, was shortlisted for the Vodafone Crossword Book Award 2008, while her academic book *Empires of the Mind* (OUP India, 2006), won the SHARP de Long Book Prize for that year. She has scripted the graphic novel version of Sunil Gangopadhyay's first Kakababu adventure, titled *Incredible Splendour* and published by Starmark. She is currently working on a science fiction novel called Antisense and a book of short stories called Ashqabad. She teaches English at Jadavpur University.

Sheena Misra Ghosh is a consultant psychologist at the leading hospitals in Kolkata. She is also an expert trainer who has worked with corporates including Coca Cola India and IIM Calcutta. She has been a school psychologist at leading educational institutions such as St. Joseph's College and Don Bosco School. Sheena is also a part of Society for Nature, Education and Health (SNEH), a Kolkata-based NGO. As a senior counselor there, she has extensive experience working with children who have behaviourial problems and disabilities, and adolescents facing the challenges of being a teenager. Her work at SNEH also involves leading workshops at schools and colleges where she teaches the youth about anger management, stress and anxiety, effective study strategies, exam phobia and other relevant issues.

Shikha Uberoi is a former top 100 WTA Tour tennis player, Asian Games Silver Medalist, India number 1, Fed Cup India leader (#1 and 2 in India). She was the first Indian woman to qualify and reach the second round of the US Open in 2004, was in the top 10 fastest servers in the world. She was also Zee Astitva Athlete of the Year in 2007. She earned her Bachelor's degree from Princeton University and graduated with high academic standing while winning Princeton's prestigious Kit Harris Memorial Award for Leadership and Ethics. She launched her media and lifestyle company, SDU Seva, Inc. in 2013 and is currently creating and producing international social issue television shows. She speaks on female empowerment through sport at both Indian and international conferences and has recently been invited to sit on the board of directors of the World Economic Forum's Global Shapers Initiative for Bhopal. She is also a news and sports presenter and coaches all levels of tennis and fitness.

Suhasini Haidar is Foreign Affairs editor and prime time anchor for India's leading 24-hr English news channel CNN-IBN, She also hosts the signature show, World View with

Suhasini Haidar (www.ibnlive.com/worldview) and the Power of 49 on women's issues. She is a regular columnist on Indian Foreign Policy and Strategic Issues for national dailies. Over the course of her 18 year reporting career, Suhasini has covered challenging stories and conflicts from diverse regions including Pakistan, Sri Lanka, Libya, Lebanon and Syria. In India, she has covered the foreign affairs beat for over a decade. Suhasini was part of the CNN team that won the Columbia-Dupont Broadcast Journalism Award in 2005 for coverage of the tsunami in India. Suhasini earned a Bachelor's degree at Lady Shriram College in Delhi, and then completed her Masters in Broadcast Journalism at Boston University's College of Communication, USA. She lives in Delhi with her husband Nadim and her two daughters Ava Mumtaz and Maya Mehr.

Tanusree Shankar is the choreographer and the chief inspiration of the troupe bearing her name. Tanusree, who trained for seven years under Amala Shankar, has developed a kind of choreography based on the Shankar technique of New Dance, following the path shown by Uday Shankar. Tanusree has handled the choreography for several prestigious international conferences, festivals and mega events, including the Asian Games, the Festival of India in the USSR and the Wills World Cup Cricket Championships. In 2008, she choreographed an Indo-French Ballet called "Padmavati" (Paris Opera) in Paris with international artistes together with 25 dancers from her troupe. The opera was directed by renowned Indian film maker, Sanjay Leela Bhansali. Later, the opera was also presented in Spoleto, Italy. Tanusree received the Sangeet Natak Akademi Award in 2011 for her contribution towards Creative and Experimental Dance. She has choreographed for numerous fashion shows and films in addition to the ballets. Her dance company has toured extensively to more than 40 countries, performing at prestigious theatres, such as Carnegie Hall in New York, Kennedy Centre in Washington D.C. and Queen Elizabeth Hall in London.

References

http://ngm.nationalgeographic.com/print/2011/10/teenage-brains/dobbs-text

Christopher Daddis. Desire for Increased Autonomy and Adolescents' Perceptions of Peer Autonomy: "Everyone Else Can; Why Can't I?". *Child Development*, 2011; DOI: 10.1111/j.1467-8624.2011.01587.x

http://www.sciencedaily.com/releases/2011/05/110511074758.htm

https://www.princeton.edu/futureofchildren/publications/docs/09_02_02.pdf

http://www.telegraph.co.uk/education/educationopinion/10035473/The-importance-of-instilling-a-need-to-read.html

http://www.cedu.niu.edu/~shumow/iit/forreview/GoalSettingForTeens.pdf

http://greatergood.berkeley.edu/article/item/how_to_help_kids_overcome_fear_of_failure

http://www.bbc.co.uk/science/humanbody/mind/articles/emotions/teenagers/love.shtml

http://www.apa.org/monitor/2012/02/friends.aspx

http://www.bristol.ac.uk/cmpo/publications/bulletin/summer11/barcellos.pdf

http://www.theatlantic.com/international/archive/2013/03/the-huge-cost-of-indias-discrimination-against-women/274115/

http://www.gulabigang.in/

http://www.livescience.com/26740-peers-girls-body-image.html

http://www.ncbi.nlm.nih.gov/pmc/articles/PMC3214444/

http://www.npr.org/blogs/health/2014/04/04/298771047/could-a-barbie-get-real-what-a-healthy-fashion-doll-looks-like

http://family.go.com/parenting/pkg-teen/article-773377-identifying-with-role-models-t/

http://www.jhsph.edu/research/centers-and-institutes/center-for-adolescent-health/_includes/Interactive%20Guide.pdf

http://family.go.com/parenting/pkg-teen/article-779137-teens-with-borderline-personality-disorders-t/

http://education.byu.edu/youcandothis/teen_tantrums.html

http://seattletimes.com/html/health/2002163863_healthteen moods30.html

http://www.bbc.com/news/magazine-24081841

http://planindia.org/about-plan/media-centre/news/plan-india-on-the-instances-of-growing-sexual-violence-against-girls-and-women/

http://www.childlineindia.org.in/Dealing-with-Child-Sexual-Abuse-Disclosures.htm

http://articles.chicagotribune.com/2011-12-13/features/sc-fam-1213-parenthood-overplan-20111213_1_overbooked-teenager-parent-s-guide-parents-limit

https://secure.ihaveaplaniowa.gov/Home/Article.aspx?level=3XAP2FPAX6J7I3kztATGuYyXAP2BPAXDahIQXAP3DPAXXAP3DPAX&articleId=IGeYH2kUApurN7JfmoFVeQXAP3DPAXXAP3DPAX

http://childdevelopmentinfo.com/child-teen-health/child_teen_safety_information

http://www.aap.org/en-us/about-the-aap/aap-press-room/news-features-and-safety-tips/pages/Talking-to-Kids-and-Teens-About-Social-Media-and-Sexting.aspx

http://www.linkedin.com/today/post/article/20130807204725-489685-raising-a-compassionate-child-in-the-age-of-entitlement